CLASSIC SCOTTISH
SHORT STORIES

Classic Scottish Short Stories

COLLECTED AND INTRODUCED

BY

Angus Black

NEW ENGLISH LIBRARY
TIMES MIRROR

An NEL Original
This collection © New English Library, 1972

*

FIRST NEL PAPERBACK EDITION MAY 1972

*

NEL Books are published by
New English Library Limited from Barnard's Inn, Holborn, London. E.C.1.
Made and printed in Great Britain by Hunt Barnard Printing Ltd., Aylesbury, Bucks.

45001243 3

CONTENTS

INTRODUCTION

There is no doubt in my mind that some of the best pieces of short fiction ever written have originated in Scotland – I refuse to use that slightly derogatory expression 'North Of The Border' as though we were some kind of English annexe, tacked on as an afterthought.

I have delved deep into my own collection and brought together eleven of the very best stories. Two of the best-loved Scottish authors – Sir Walter Scott and Robert Louis Stevenson – are each represented by two stories.

The remainder of the anthology is composed of some of the most brilliant pieces of short fiction by authors who are only slightly less-known. My own favourite is W. E. Aytoun's 'The Man In The Bell' but it's difficult to pick just one favourite out of such a glittering company.

Angus Black
Glasgow, February, 1972

ROBERT LOUIS STEVENSON

THE SIRE DE MALÉTROIT'S DOOR

DENIS DE BEAULIEU was not yet two-and-twenty, but he counted himself a grown man, and a very accomplished cavalier into the bargain. Lads were early formed in that rough, warfaring epoch; and when one has been in a pitched battle and a dozen raids, has killed one's man in an honourable fashion, and knows a thing or two of strategy and mankind, a certain swagger in the gait is surely to be pardoned. He had put up his horse with due care, and supped with due deliberation; and then, in a very agreeable frame of mind, went out to pay a visit in the grey of the evening. It was not a very wise proceeding on the young man's part. He would have done better to remain beside the fire or go decently to bed. For the town was full of the troops of Burgundy and England under a mixed command; and though Denis was there on safe-conduct, his safe-conduct was like to serve him little on a chance encounter.

It was September 1429; the weather had fallen sharp; a flighty piping wind, laden with showers, beat about the township; and the dead leaves ran riot along the streets. Here and there a window was already lighted up; and the noise of men-at-arms making merry over supper within, came forth in fits and was swallowed up and carried away by the wind. The night fell swiftly; the flag of England, fluttering on the spire-top, grew ever fainter and fainter against the flying clouds – a black speck like a swallow in the tumultuous, leaden chaos of the sky. As the night fell the wind rose, and began to hoot under archways and roar amid the tree-tops in the valley below the town.

Denis de Beaulieu walked fast and was soon knocking at his friend's door; but though he promised himself to stay only a little while and make an early return, his welcome was so pleasant, and he found so much to delay him, that it was already long past midnight before he said good-bye upon the threshold. The wind had fallen again in the meanwhile; the night was as black as the grave; not a star, nor a glimmer of moonshine, slipped through the canopy of cloud. Denis was ill-acquainted with the intricate lanes of

9

Chateau Landon; even by daylight he had found some trouble in picking his way; and in this absolute darkness he soon lost it altogether. He was certain of one thing only – to keep mounting the hill; for his friend's house lay at the lower end, or tail, of Chateau Landon, while the inn was up at the head, under the great church spire. With this clue to go upon he stumbled and groped forward, now breathing more freely in open places where there was a good slice of sky overhead, now feeling along the wall in stifling closes. It is an eerie and mysterious position to be thus submerged in opaque blackness in an almost unknown town. The silence is terrifying in its possibilities. The touch of cold window bars to the exploring hand startles the man like the touch of a toad; the inequalities of the pavement shake his heart into his mouth; a piece of denser darkness threatens an ambuscade or a chasm in the pathway; and where the air is brighter, the houses put on strange and bewildering appearances, as if to lead him farther from his way. For Denis, who had to regain his inn without attracting notice, there was real danger as well as mere discomfort in the walk; and he went warily and boldly at once, and at every corner paused to make an observation.

He had been for some time threading a lane so narrow that he could touch a wall with either hand, when it began to open out and go sharply downward. Plainly this lay no longer in the direction of his inn; but the hope of a little more light tempted him forward to reconnoitre. The land ended in a terrace with a bartizan wall, which gave an outlook between high houses, as out of an embrasure, into the valley lying dark and formless several hundred feet below. Denis looked down, and could discern a few tree-tops waving and a single speck of brightness where the river ran across a weir. The weather was clearing up, and the sky had lightened, so as to show the outline of the heavier clouds and the dark margin of the hills. By the uncertain glimmer, the house on his left hand should be a place of some pretensions; it was surmounted by several pinnacles and turret-tops; the round stern of a chapel, with a fringe of flying buttresses, projected boldly from the main block; and the door was sheltered under a deep porch carved with figures and overhung by two long gargoyles. The windows of the chapel gleamed through their intricate tracery with a light as of many tapers, and threw out the buttresses and the peaked roof in a more intense blackness against the sky. It was plainly the hotel of some great family of the neighbourhood; and as it reminded Denis of a town house of his own at Bourges, he stood for some time gazing up at it and mentally gauging the skill of the architects and the

10

consideration of the two families.

There seemed to be no issue to the terrace but the lane by which he had reached it; he could only retrace his steps, but he had gained some notion of his whereabouts, and hoped by this means to hit the main thoroughfare and speedily regain the inn. He was reckoning without that chapter of accidents which was to make this night memorable above all others in his career; for he had not gone back above a hundred yards before he saw a light coming to meet him, and heard loud voices speaking together in the echoing narrows of the lane. It was a party of men-at-arms going the night round with torches. Denis assured himself that they had all been making free with the wine-bowl, and were in no mood to be particular about safe-conducts or the niceties of chivalrous war. It was as like as not that they would kill him like a dog and leave him where he fell. The situation was inspiriting but nervous. Their own torches would conceal him from sight, he reflected; and he hoped that they would drown the noise of his footsteps with their own empty voices. If he were but silent and fleet he might evade their notice altogether.

Unfortunately, as he turned to beat a retreat, his foot rolled upon a pebble; he fell against the wall with an ejaculation, and his sword rang loudly on the stones. Two or three voices demanded who went there – some in French, some in English; but Denis made no reply, and ran the faster down the lane. Once upon the terrace, he paused to look back. They still kept calling after him, and just then began to double the pace in pursuit, with a considerable clank of armour, and great tossing of the torchlight to and fro in the narrow jaws of the passage.

Denis cast a look around and darted into the porch. There he might escape observation, or – if that were too much to expect – was in a capital posture whether for parley or defence. So thinking, he drew his sword and tried to set his back against the door. To his surprise, it yielded behind his weight; and though he turned in a moment, continued to swing back on oiled and noiseless hinges, until it stood wide open on a black interior. When things fall out opportunely for the person concerned, he is not apt to be critical about the how or why, his own immediate personal convenience seeming a sufficient reason for the strangest oddities and revolutions in our sublunary things; and so Denis, without a moment's hesitation, stepped within and partly closed the door behind him to conceal his place of refuge. Nothing was further from his thoughts than to close it altogether; but for some inexplicable reason – perhaps by a spring or a weight – the ponderous mass of oak whipped itself out of his fingers and clanked to, with a formidable rumble and a noise like the falling of an automatic bar.

The round, at that very moment, debouched upon the terrace and proceeded to summon him with shouts and curses. He heard them ferreting in the dark corners; the stock of a lance even rattled along the outer surface of the door behind which he stood; but these gentlemen were in too high a humour to be long delayed, and soon made off down a corkscrew pathway which had escaped Denis's observation, and passed out of sight and hearing along the battlements of the town.

Denis breathed again. He gave them a few minutes' grace for fear of accidents, and then groped about for some means of opening the door and slipping forth again. The inner surface was quite smooth, not a handle, not a moulding, not a projection of any sort. He got his finger-nails round the edges and pulled, but the mass was immovable. He shook it, it was as firm as a rock. Denis de Beaulieu frowned and gave vent to a little noiseless whistle. What ailed the door? he wondered. Why was it open? How came it to shut so easily and so effectually after him? There was something obscure and underhand about all this that was little to the young man's fancy. It looked like a snare; and yet who could suppose a snare in such a quiet by-street and in a house of so prosperous and even noble an exterior? And yet – snare or no snare, intentionally or unintentionally – here he was, prettily trapped; and for the life of him he could see no way out of it again. The darkness began to weigh upon him. He gave ear; all was silent without, but within and close by he seemed to catch a faint sighing, a faint sobbing rustle, a little stealthy creak – as though many persons were at his side, holding themselves quite still, and governing even their respiration with the extreme of slyness. The idea went to his vitals with a shock, and he faced about suddenly as if to defend his life. Then, for the first time, he became aware of a light about the level of his eyes and at some distance in the interior of the house – a vertical thread of light, widening towards the bottom, such as might escape between two wings of arras over a doorway. To see anything was a relief to Denis; it was like a piece of solid ground to a man labouring in a morass; his mind seized upon it with avidity; and he stood staring at it and trying to piece together some logical conception of his surroundings. Plainly there was a flight of steps ascending from his own level to that of this illuminated doorway; and indeed he thought he could make out another thread of light, as fine as a needle and as faint as phosphorescence, which might very well be reflected along the polished wood of a handrail. Since he had begun to suspect that he was not alone, his heart had continued to beat with smothering violence, and an intolerable desire for action of any sort had possessed itself of his spirit. He was in deadly peril, he believed. What could be more natural than to mount the staircase, lift the curtain, and confront his difficulty at once? At least he would be dealing with something tangible; at least he would be no longer in the dark. He stepped slowly forward with outstretched hands, until his foot struck the bottom step; then he rapidly scaled the stairs, stood for a moment to compose his expression, lifted the arras and went in.

He found himself in a large apartment of polished stone. There were three doors; one in each of three sides; all similarly curtained with tapestry. The fourth side was occupied by two large windows and a great stone chimney-piece, carved with the arms of the Malétroits. Denis recognised the bearings, and was gratified to find himself in such good hands. The room was strongly illuminated; but it contained little furniture except a heavy table and a chair or two, the hearth was innocent of fire, and the pavement was but sparsely strewn with rushes clearly many days old.

On a high chair beside the chimney, and directly facing Denis as he entered, sat a little old gentleman in a fur tippet. He sat with his legs crossed and his hands folded, and a cup of spiced wine stood by his elbow on a bracket on the wall. His countenance had a strongly masculine cast; not properly human, but such as we see in the bull, the goat, or the domestic boar; something equivocal and wheedling, something greedy, brutal, and dangerous. The upper lip was inordinately full, as though swollen by a blow or a tooth-ache; and the smile, the peaked eyebrows, and the small, strong eyes were quaintly and almost comically evil in expression. Beautiful white hair hung straight all round his head, like a saint's, and fell in a single curl upon the tippet. His beard and moustache were the pink of venerable sweetness. Age, probably in consequence of inordinate precautions, had left no mark upon his hands, and the Malétroit hand was famous. It would be difficult to imagine anything at once so fleshy and so delicate in design; the taper, sensual fingers were like those of one of Leonardo's women; the fork of the thumb made a dimpled protuberance when closed; the nails were perfectly shaped, and of a dead, surprising whiteness. It rendered his aspect tenfold more redoubtable, that a man with hands like these should keep them devoutly folded in his lap like a virgin martyr – that a man with so intense and startling an expression of face should sit patiently on his seat and contemplate people with an unwinking stare, like a god, or a god's statue. His quiescence seemed ironical and treacherous, it fitted so poorly with his looks.

13

Such was Alain, Sire de Malétroit.

Denis and he looked silently at each other for a second or two.

'Pray step in,' said the Sire de Malétroit. 'I have been expecting you all the evening.'

He had not risen, but he accompanied his words with a smile, and a slight but courteous inclination of the head. Partly from the smile, partly from the strange musical murmur which which the Sire prefaced his observation, Denis felt a strong shudder of disgust go through his marrow. And what with disgust and honest confusion of mind, he could scarcely get words together in reply.

'I fear,' he said, 'that this is a double accident. I am not the person you suppose me. It seems you were looking for a visit; but for my part, nothing was further from my thoughts – nothing could be more contrary to my wishes – than this intrusion.'

'Well, well,' replied the old gentleman indulgently, 'here you are, which is the main point. Seat yourself, my friend, and put yourself entirely at your ease. We shall arrange our little affairs presently.'

Denis perceived that the matter was still complicated with some misconception, and he hastened to continue his explanations.

'Your door . . . ' he began.

'About my door?' asked the other, raising his peaked eyebrows. 'A little piece of ingenuity.' And he shrugged his shoulders. 'A hospitable fancy! By your own account, you were not desirous of making my acquaintance. We old people look for such reluctance now and then; and when it touches our honour, we cast about until we find some way of overcoming it. You arrive uninvited, but believe me, very welcome.'

'You persist in error, sir,' said Denis. 'There can be no question between you and me. I am a stranger in this countryside. My name is Denis, damoiseau de Beaulieu. If you see me in your house, it is only – '

'My young friend,' interrupted the other, 'you will permit me to have my own ideas on that subject. They probably differ from yours at the present moment,' he added with a leer, 'but time will show which of us is in the right.'

Denis was convinced he had to do with a lunatic. He seated himself with a shrug, content to wait the upshot; and a pause ensued, during which he thought he could distinguish a hurried gabbling as of prayer from behind the arras immediately opposite him. Sometimes there seemed to be but one person engaged, sometimes two; and the vehemence of the voice, low as it was, seemed to indicate either great haste or an agony of spirit. It occurred to him that this piece of tapestry covered the entrance to the chapel he had noticed from without.

The old gentleman meanwhile surveyed Denis from head to foot with a smile, and from time to time emitted little noises like a bird or a mouse, which seemed to indicate a high degree of satisfaction. This state of matters became rapidly insupportable; and Denis, to put an end to it, remarked politely that the wind had gone down.

The old gentleman fell into a fit of silent laughter, so prolonged and violent that he became quite red in the face. Denis got upon his feet at once, and put his hat on with a flourish.

'Sir,' he said, 'if you are in your wits, you have affronted me grossly. If you are out of them, I flatter myself I can find better employment for my brains than to talk with lunatics. My conscience is clear; you have made a fool of me from the first moment; you have refused to hear my explanations; and now there is no power under God will make me stay here any longer; and if I cannot make my way out in a more decent fashion, I will hack your door in pieces with my sword.'

The Sire de Malétroit raised his right hand and wagged it at Denis with the fore and little fingers extended.

'My dear nephew,' he said, 'sit down.'

'Nephew!' retorted Denis, 'you lie in your throat'; and he snapped his fingers in his face.

'Sit down, you rogue!' cried the old gentleman, in a sudden, harsh voice, like the barking of a dog. 'Do you fancy,' he went on, 'that when I had made my little contrivance for the door I had stopped short with that? If you prefer to be bound hand and foot till your bones ache, rise and try to go away. If you choose to remain a free young buck, agreeably conversing with an old gentleman – why, sit where you are in peace, and God be with you.'

'Do you mean I am a prisoner?' demanded Denis.

'I state the facts,' replied the other. 'I would rather leave the conclusion to yourself.'

Denis sat down again. Externally he managed to keep pretty calm; but within, he was now boiling with anger, now chilled with apprehension. He no longer felt convinced that he was dealing with a madman. And if the old gentleman was sane, what, in God's name, had he to look for? What absurd or tragical adventure had befallen him? What countenance was he to assume?

While he was thus unpleasantly reflecting, the arras that overhung the chapel door was raised, and a tall priest in his robes came forth and, giving a long, keen stare at Denis, said something in an undertone to Sire de Malétroit.

'She is in a better frame of spirit?' asked the latter.

'She is more resigned, messire,' replied the priest.

'Now the Lord help her, she is hard to please!' sneered the old gentleman. 'A likely stripling – not ill-born – and of her own choosing, too? Why, what more would the jade have?'

'The situation is not usual for a young damsel,' said the other, 'and somewhat trying to her blushes.'

'She should have thought of that before she began the dance? It was none of my choosing, God knows that: but since she is in it, by our lady, she shall carry it to the end.' And then addressing Denis, 'Monsieur de Beaulieu,' he asked, 'may I present you to my niece? She has been waiting your arrival, I may say, with even greater impatience than myself.'

Denis had resigned himself with a good grace – all he desired was to know the worst of it as speedily as possible; so he rose at once, and bowed in acquiescence. The Sire de Malétroit followed his example and limped with the assistance of the chaplain's arm, towards the chapel-door. The priest pulled aside the arras, and all three entered. The building had considerable architectural pretensions. A light groining sprang from six stout columns, and hung down in two rich pendants from the centre of the vault. The place terminated behind the altar in a round end, embossed and honeycombed with a superfluity of ornament in relief, and pierced by many little windows shaped like stars, trefoils, or wheels. These windows were imperfectly glazed, so that the night air circulated freely in the chapel. The tapers, of which there must have been half a hundred burning on the âltar, were unmercifully blown about; and the light went through many different phases of brilliancy and semi-eclipse. On the steps in front of the altar knelt a young girl richly attired as a bride. A chill settled over Denis as he observed her costume; he fought with desperate energy against the conclusion that was being thrust upon his mind; it could not – it should not – be as he feared.

'Blanche,' said the Sire, in his most flute-like tones, 'I have brought a friend to see you, my little girl; turn round and give him your pretty hand. It is good to be devout; but it is necessary to be polite, my niece.'

The girl rose to her feet and turned towards the new-comers. She moved all of a piece; and shame and exhaustion were expressed in every line of her fresh young body; and she held her head down and kept her eyes upon the pavement, as she came slowly forward. In the course of her advance, her eyes fell upon Denis de Beaulieu's feet – feet of which he was justly vain, be it remarked, and wore in the most elegant accoutrement even while travelling. She paused –

started, as if his yellow boots had conveyed some shocking meaning – and glanced suddenly up into the wearer's countenance. Their eyes met; shame gave place to horror and terror in her looks; the blood left her lips; with a piercing scream she covered her face with her hands and sank upon the chapel floor.

'That is not the man!' she cried. 'My uncle; that is not the man!'

The Sire de Malétroit chirped agreeably. 'Of course not,' he said, 'I expected as much. It was so unfortunate you could not remember his name.'

'Indeed,' she cried, 'indeed, I have never seen this person till this moment – I have never so much as set eyes upon him – I never wish to see him again. Sir,' she said, turning to Denis, 'if you are a gentleman, you will bear me out. Have I ever seen you – have you ever seen me – before this accursed hour?'

'To speak for myself, I have never had that pleasure,' answered the young man. 'This is the first time, messire, that I have met with your engaging niece.'

The old gentleman shrugged his shoulders.

'I am distressed to hear it,' he said. 'But it is never too late to begin. I had little more acquaintance with my own late lady ere I married her; which proves,' he added, with a grimace, 'that these impromptu marriages may often produce an excellent understanding in the long-run. As the bridegroom is to have a voice in the matter, I will give him two hours to make up for lost time before we proceed with the ceremony.' And he turned towards the door, followed by the clergyman.

The girl was on her feet in a moment. 'My uncle ,you cannot be in earnest,' she said. 'I declare before God I will stab myself rather than be forced on that young man. The heart rises at it; God forbids such marriages; you dishonour your white hair. Oh, my uncle, pity me! There is not a woman in all the world but would prefer death to such a nuptial. Is it possible,' she added, faltering – 'is it possible that you do not believe me – that you still think this' – and she pointed at Denis with a tremor of anger and contempt – 'that you still think *this* to be the man?'

'Frankly,' said the old gentleman, pausing on the threshold, 'I do. But let me explain to you once for all, Blanche de Malétroit, my way of thinking about this affair. When you took it into your head to dishonour my family and the name that I have borne, in peace and war, for more than threescore years, you forfeited, not only the right to question my designs, but that of looking me in the face. If your father had been alive, he would have spat on you and turned you out of doors. His was the hand of iron. You may bless your God you have only to deal with the hand of velvet, mademoiselle. It was my duty to get you married without delay. Out of pure goodwill, I have tried to find your own gallant for you. And I believe I have succeeded. But before God and all the holy angels, Blanche de Malétroit, if I have not, I care not one jackstraw. So let me recommend you to be polite to our young friend; for upon my word, your next groom may be less appetising.'

And with that he went out, with the chaplain at his heels; and the arras fell behind the pair.

The girl turned upon Denis with flashing eyes.

'And what, sir,' she demanded, 'may be the meaning of all this?'

'God knows,' returned Denis gloomily. 'I am a prisoner in this house, which seems full of mad people. More I know not; and nothing do I understand.'

'And pray how came you here?' she asked.

He told her as briefly as he could. 'For the rest,' he added, 'perhaps you will follow my example, and tell me the answer to all these riddles, and what, in God's name, is like to be the end of it.'

She stood silent for a little, and he could see her lips tremble and her tearless eyes burn with a feverish lustre. Then she pressed her forehead in both hands.

'Alas, how my head aches!' she said wearily – 'to say nothing of my poor heart! But it is due to you to know my story, unmaidenly as it must seem. I am called Blanche de Malétroit: I have been without father or mother for – oh! for as long as I can recollect, and indeed I have been most unhappy all my life. Three months ago a young captain began to stand near me every day in church. I could see that I pleased him; I am much to blame, but I was so glad that anyone should love me; and when he passed me a letter, I took it home with me and read it with great pleasure. Since that time he has written many. He was so anxious to speak with me, poor fellow! and kept asking me to leave the door open some evening that we might have two words upon the stair. For he knew how much my uncle trusted me.' She gave something like a sob at that, and it was a moment before she could go on. 'My uncle is a hard man, but he is very shrewd,' she said at last. 'He has performed many feats in war, and was a great person at court, and much trusted by Queen Isabeau in old days. How he came to suspect me I cannot tell; but it is hard to keep anything from his knowledge; and this morning, as we came from mass, he took my hand in his, forced it open, and read my little billet, walking by my side all the while. When he had finished, he gave it back to me with great politeness. It contained another request to have the door left open;

18

and this has been the ruin of us all. My uncle kept me strictly in my room until evening, and then ordered me to dress myself as you see me – a hard mockery for a young girl, do you not think so? I suppose, when he could not prevail with me to tell him the young captain's name, he must have laid a trap for him: into which, alas! you have fallen in the anger of God. I looked for much confusion; for how could I tell whether he was willing to take me for his wife on these sharp terms? He might have been trifling with me from the first; or I might have made myself too cheap in his eyes. But truly I had not looked for such a shameful punishment as this! I could not think that God would let a girl be so disgraced before a young man. And now I have told you all; and I can scarcely hope that you will not despise me.'

Denis made her a respectful inclination.

'Madam,' he said, 'you have honoured me by your confidence. It remains for me to prove that I am not unworthy of the honour. Is Messire de Malétroit at hand?'

'I believe he is writing in the salle without,' she answered.

'May I lead you thither, madam?' asked Denis, offering his hand with his most courtly bearing.

She accepted it; and the pair passed out of the chapel, Blanche in a very drooping and shamefast condition, but Denis strutting and ruffling in the consciousness of a mission, and the boyish certainty of accomplishing it with honour.

The Sire de Malétroit rose to meet them with an ironical obeisance.

'Sir,' said Denis, with the grandest possible air, 'I believe I am to have some say in the matter of this marriage; and let me tell you at once, I will be no party to forcing the inclination of this young lady. Had it been freely offered to me, I should have been proud to accept her hand, for I perceive she is as good as she is beautiful; but as things are, I have now the honour, messire, of refusing.'

Blanche looked at him with gratitude in her eyes; but the old gentleman only smiled and smiled until his smile grew positively sickening to Denis.

'I am afraid,' he said, 'Monsieur de Beaulieu, that you do not perfectly understand the choice I have to offer you. Follow me, I beseech you, to this window.' And he led the way to one of the large windows which stood open on the night. 'You observe,' he went on, 'there is an iron ring in the upper masonry, and reeved through that a very efficacious rope. Now, mark my words: if you should find your disinclination to my niece's person insurmountable, I shall have you hanged out of this window before sunrise. I shall only proceed to such an extremity with the greatest regret, you may believe me. For it is not at all your death that I desire, but my niece's establishment in life. At the same time, it must come to that if you prove obstinate. Your family, Monsieur de Beaulieu, is very well in its way; but if you sprang from Charlemagne you should not refuse the hand of a Malétroit with impunity – not if she had been as common as the Paris road – not if she were as hideous as the gargoyle over my door. Neither my niece nor you, nor my own private feelings, move me at all in this matter. The honour of my house had been compromised; I believe you to be the guilty person; at least you are now in the secret; and you can hardly wonder if I request you to wipe out the stain. If you will not, your blood be on your own head! It will be no great satisfaction to me to have your interesting relics kicking their heels in the breeze below my windows; but half a loaf is better than no bread, and if I cannot cure the dishonour, I shall at least stop the scandal.'

There was a pause.

'I believe there are other ways of settling such imbroglios among gentlemen,' said Denis. 'You wear a sword, and I hear you have used it with distinction.'

The Sire de Malétroit made a signal to the chaplain, who crossed the room with long silent strides and raised the arras over the third of the three doors. It was only a moment before he let it fall again; but Denis had time to see a dusky passage full of armed men.

'When I was a little younger, I should have been delighted to honour you, Monsieur de Beaulieu,' said Sire Alain; 'but I am now too old. Faithful retainers are the sinews of age, and I must employ the strength I have. This is one of the hardest things to swallow as a man grows up in years; but with a little patience, even this becomes habitual. You and the lady seem to prefer the salle for what remains of your two hours; and as I have no desire to cross your preference, I shall resign it to your use with all the pleasure in the world. No haste!' he added, holding up his hand, as he saw a dangerous look come into Denis de Beaulieu's face. 'If your mind revolts against hanging, it will be time enough two hours hence to throw yourself out of the window or upon the pikes of my retainers. Two hours of life are always two hours. A great many things may turn up in even as little a while as that. And, besides, if I understand her appearance, my niece has still something to say to you. You will not disfigure your last hours by a want of politeness to a lady?'

Denis looked at Blanche, and she made him an imploring gesture.

It is likely that the old gentleman was hugely pleased at this symptom of an understanding; for he smiled on both, and added sweetly: 'If you will give me your word of honour, Monsieur de Beaulieu, to await my return at the end of the two hours before attempting anything desperate, I shall withdraw my retainers, and let you speak in greater privacy with mademoiselle.'

Denis again glanced at the girl, who seemed to beseech him to agree.

'I give you my word of honour,' he said.

Messire de Malétroit bowed, and proceeded to limp about the apartment, clearing his throat the while with that odd musical chirp which had already grown so irritating in the ears of Denis de Beaulieu. He first possessed himself of some papers which lay upon the table; then he went to the mouth of the passage and appeared to give an order to the men behind the arras; and lastly, he hobbled out through the door by which Denis had come in, turning upon the threshold to address a last smiling bow to the young couple, and followed by the chaplain with a hand-lamp.

No sooner were they alone than Blanche advanced towards Denis with her hands extended. Her face was flushed and excited, and her eyes shone with tears.

'You shall not die!' she cried, 'you shall marry me after all.'

'You seem to think, madam,' replied Denis, 'that I stand much in fear of death.'

'Oh no, no,' she said, 'I see you are no poltroon. It is for my own sake – I could not bear to have you slain for such a scruple.'

'I am afraid,' returned Denis, 'that you underrate the difficulty, madam. What you may be too generous to refuse, I may be too proud to accept. In a moment of noble feeling towards me, you forgot what you perhaps owe to others.'

He had the decency to keep his eyes upon the floor as he said this, and after he had finished, so as not to spy upon her confusion. She stood silent for a moment, then walked suddenly away, and falling on her uncle's chair, fairly burst out sobbing. Denis was in the acme of embarrassment. He looked round, as if to seek for inspiration, and seeing a stool, plumped down upon it for something to do. There he sat, playing with the guard of his rapier, and wishing himself dead a thousand times over, and buried in the nastiest kitchen-heap in France. His eyes wandered round the apartment, but found nothing to arrest them. There were such wide spaces between the furniture, the light fell so baldly and cheerlessly over all, the dark outside air looked in so coldly through the windows, that he thought he had never seen a church so vast, nor a tomb so melancholy. The regular sobs of Blanche de Malé-troit measured out the time like the ticking of a clock. He read the device upon the shield over and over again, until his eyes became obscured; he stared into shadowy corners until he imagined they were swarming with horrible animals; and every now and again he awoke with a start, to remember that his last two hours were running, and death was on the march.

Oftener and oftener, as the time went on, did his glance settle on the girl herself. Her face was bowed forward and covered with her hands, and she was shaken at intervals by the convulsive hiccup of grief. Even thus she was not an unpleasant object to dwell upon, so plump and yet so fine, with a warm brown skin, and the most beautiful hair, Denis thought, in the whole world of womankind. Her hands were like her uncle's; but they were more in place at the end of her young arms, and looked infinitely soft and caressing. He remembered how her blue eyes had shone upon him, full of anger, pity, and innocence. And the more he dwelt on her perfections, the uglier death looked, and the more deeply was he smitten with penitence at her continued tears. Now he felt that no man could have the courage to leave a world which contained so beautiful a creature; and now he would have given forty minutes of his last hour to have unsaid his cruel speech.

Suddenly a hoarse and ragged peal of cockcrow rose to their ears from the dark valley below the windows. And this shattering noise in the silence of all around was like a light in a dark place, and shook them both out of their reflections.

'Alas, can I do nothing to help you?' she said, looking up.

'Madam,' replied Denis, with a fine irrelevancy, 'if I have said anything to wound you, believe me, it was for your own sake and not for mine.'

She thanked him with a tearful look.

'I feel your position cruelly,' he went on. 'The world has been bitter hard on you. Your uncle is a disgrace to mankind. Believe me, madam, there is no young gentleman in all France but would be glad of my opportunity, to die in doing you a momentary service.'

'I know already that you can be very brave and generous,' she answered. 'What I *want* to know is whether I can serve you – now or afterwards,' she added, with a quaver.

'Most certainly,' he answered, with a smile. 'Let me sit beside you as if I were a friend, instead of a foolish intruder; try to forget how awkwardly we are placed to one another; make my last moments go pleasantly; and you will do me the chief service possible.'

'You are very gallant,' she added, with a yet deeper sadness … 'very gallant … and it somehow pains me. But draw nearer, if you please; and if you find anything to say to me, you will at least make certain of a very friendly listener. Ah! Monsieur de Beaulieu,' she broke forth – 'ah! Monsieur de Beaulieu, how can I look you in the face?' And she fell to weeping again with a renewed effusion.

'Madam,' said Denis, taking her hand in both of his, 'reflect on the little time I have before me, and the great bitterness into which I am cast by the sight of your distress. Spare me, in my last moments, the spectacle of what I cannot cure even with the sacrifice of my life.'

'I am very selfish,' answered Blanche. 'I will be braver, Monsieur de Beaulieu, for your sake. But think if I can do you no kindness in the future – if you have no friends to whom I could carry your adieux. Charge me as heavily as you can; every burden will lighten, by so little, the invaluable gratitude I owe you. Put it in my power to do something more for you than weep.'

'My mother is married again, and has a young family to care for. My brother Guichard will inherit my fiefs; and if I am not in error, that will content him amply for my death. Life is a little vapour that passeth away, as we are told by those in holy orders. When a man is in a fair way and sees all life open in front of him, he seems to himself to make a very important figure in the world. His horse whinnies to him; the trumpets blow and the girls look out of window as he rides into town before his company; he receives many assurances of trust and regard – sometimes by express in a letter–sometimes face to face, with persons of great consequence falling on his neck. It is not wonderful if his head is turned for a time. But once he is dead, were he as brave as Hercules or as wise as Solomon, he is soon forgotten. It is not ten years since my father fell, with many other knights around him, in a very fierce en-counter, and I do not think that any one of them, nor so much as the name of the fight is now remembered. No, no, madam, the nearer you come to it, you see that death is a dark and dusty corner, where a man gets into his tomb and has the door shut after him till the judgement day. I have few friends just now, and once I am dead I shall have none.'

'Ah, Monsieur de Beaulieu!' she exclaimed, 'you forget Blanche de Malétroit.'

'You have a sweet nature, madam, and you are pleased to estimate a little service far beyond its worth.'

'It is not that,' she answered. 'You mistake me if you think I am so easily touched by my own concerns. I say so, because you are the noblest man I have ever met; because I recognise in you a spirit that would have made even a common person famous in the land.'

'And yet here I die in a mousetrap – with no more noise about it than my own squealing,' answered he.

A look of pain crossed her face, and she was silent for a little while. Then a light came into her eyes, and with a smile she spoke again.

'I cannot have my champion think meanly of himself. Any one who gives his life for another will be met in Paradise by all the heralds and angels of the Lord God. And you have no such cause to hang your head. For . . . Pray, do you think me beautiful?' she asked, with a deep flush.

'Indeed, madam, I do,' he said.

'I am glad of that,' she answered heartily. 'Do you think there are many men in France who have been asked in marriage by a beautiful maiden – with her own lips – and who have refused her to her face? I know you men would half despise such a triumph; but believe me, we women know more of what is precious in love. There is nothing that should set a person higher in his own esteem; and we women would prize nothing more dearly.'

'You are very good,' he said; 'but you cannot make me forget that I was asked in pity and not for love.'

'I am not so sure of that,' she replied, holding down her head. 'Hear me to an end, Monsieur de Beaulieu. I know how you must despise me; I feel you are right to do so; I am too poor a creature to occupy one thought of your mind, although, alas! you must die for me this morning. But when I asked you to marry me, indeed, and indeed, it was because I respected and admired you, and loved you with my whole soul, from the very moment that you took my part against my uncle. If you had seen yourself, and how noble you looked, you would pity rather than despise me. And now,' she went on, hurriedly checking him with her hand, 'although I have laid aside all reserve and told you so much, remember that I know your sentiments towards me already. I would not, believe me, being nobly born, weary you with importunities into consent. I too have a pride of my own; and I declare before the holy mother of God, if you should now go back from your word already given, I would no more marry you than I would marry my uncle's groom.'

Denis smiled a little bitterly.

'It is a small love,' he said, 'that shies at a little pride.'

She made no answer, although she probably had her own thoughts.

'Come hither to the window,' he said, with a sigh. 'Here is the dawn.'

And indeed the dawn was already beginning. The hollow of the sky was full of essential daylight, colourless and clean; and the valley underneath was flooded with a grey reflection. A few thin vapours clung in the coves of the forest or lay along the winding course of the river. The scene disengaged a surprising effect of stillness, which was hardly interrupted when the cocks began once more to crow among the steadings. Perhaps the same fellow who had made so horrid a clangour in the darkness not half-an-hour before, now sent up the merriest cheer to greet the coming day. A little wind went bustling and eddying among the tree-tops underneath the windows. And still the daylight kept flooding insensibly out of the east, which was soon to grow incandescent and cast up that red-hot cannon-ball, the rising sun.

Denis looked out over all this with a bit of a shiver. He had taken her hand, and retained it in his almost unconsciously.

'Has the day begun already?' she said; and then, illogically enough: 'the night has been so long! Alas! what shall we say to my uncle when he returns?'

'What you will,' said Denis, and he pressed her fingers in his.

She was silent.

'Blanche,' he said, with a swift, uncertain, passionate utterance, 'you have seen whether I fear death. You must know well enough that I would as gladly leap out of that window into the empty air as lay a finger on you without your free and full consent. But if you care for me at all do not let me lose my life in a misapprehension; for I love you better than the whole world; and though I will die for you blithely it would be like all the joys of Paradise to live on and spend my life in your service.'

As he stopped speaking, a bell began to ring loudly in the interior of the house; and a clatter of armour in the corridor showed that the retainers were returning to their post, and the two hours were at an end.

'After all that you have heard?' she whispered, leaning towards him with her lips and eyes.

'I have heard nothing,' he replied.

'The captain's name was Florimond de Champdivers,' she said in his ear.

'I did not hear it,' he answered, taking her supple body in his arms, and covered her wet face with kisses.

A melodious chirping was audible behind, followed by a beautiful chuckle, and the voice of Messire de Malétroit wished his new nephew a good morning.

WANDERING WILLIE'S TALE

'Honest folks like me! How do ye ken whether I am honest, or what I am? I may be the deevil himsell for what ye ken, for he has power to come disguised like an angel of light; and, besides, he is a prime fiddler. He played a sonata to Corelli, ye ken.'

There was something odd in this speech, and the tone in which it was said. It seemed as if my companion was not always in his constant mind, or that he was willing to try if he could frighten me. I laughed at the extravagance of his language, however, and asked him in reply if he was fool enough to believe that the foul fiend would play so silly a masquerade.

'Ye ken little about it – little about it,' said the old man, shaking his head and beard, and knitting his brows. 'I could tell ye something about that.'

What his wife mentioned of his being a tale-teller as well as a musician now occurred to me; and as, you know, I like tales of superstition, I begged to have a specimen of his talent as we went along.

'It is very true,' said the blind man, 'that when I am tired of scraping thairm or singing ballants I whiles make a tale serve the turn among the country bodies; and I have some fearsome anes, that make the auld carlines shake on the settle, and the bits 'o bairns skirl on their minnies out frae their beds. But this that I am going to tell you was a thing that befell in our ain house in my father's time – that is, my father was then a hafflins callant; and I tell it to you, that it may be a lesson to you, that are but a young thoughtless chap, wha ye draw up wi' on a lonely road; for muckle was the dool and care that came o' 't to my gudesire.'

He commenced his tale accordingly, in a distinct narrative tone of voice, which he raised and depressed with considerable skill – at times sinking almost into a whisper, and turning his clear but sightless eyeballs upon my face, as if it had been possible for him to witness the impression which his narrative made upon my features.

I will not spare a syllable of it, although it be of the longest; so I make a dash – and begin:

Ye maun have heard of Sir Robert Redgauntlet of that Ilk, who lived in these parts before the dear years. The country will lang mind him; and our fathers used to draw breath thick if ever they heard him named. He was out wi' the Hielandmen in Montrose's time; and again he was in the hills wi' Glencairn in the saxteen hundred and fifty-twa; and sae when King Charles the Second came in, wha was in sic favour as the laird of Redgauntlet? He was knighted at Lonon Court, wi' the king's ain sword; and being a red-hot prelatist, he came down here, rampauging like a lion, with commissions of lieutenancy (and of lunacy, for what I ken), to put down a' the Whigs and Covenanters in the country. Wild wark they made of it; for the Whigs were as dour as the Cavaliers were fierce, and it was which should first tire the other. Redgauntlet was aye for the strong hand; and his name is kenn'd as wide in the country as Claverhouse's or Tam Dalyell's. Glen, nor dargle, nor mountain, nor cave could hide the puir hill-folk when Redgauntlet was out with bugle and bloodhound after them, as if they had been sae mony deer. And, troth, when they fand them, they didna make muckle mair ceremony than a Hielandman wi' a roebuck. It was just, 'Will ye tak' the test?' If not, 'Make ready – present – fire!' and there lay the recusant.

Far and wide was Sir Robert hated and feared. Men thought he had a direct compact with Satan; that he was proof against steel and that bullets happed aff his buff-coat like hailstanes from a hearth; that he had a mear that would turn a hare on the side of Carrifragauns;* and muckle to the same purpose, of whilk mair anon. The best blessing they wared on him was, 'Deil scowp wi' Redgauntlet!' He wasna a bad master to his ain folk, though, and was weel aneugh liked by his tenants; and as for the lackeys and troopers that rade at wi' him to the persecutions, as the Whigs' ca'd those killing-times, they wad hae drunken themsells blind to his health at ony time.

Now you are to ken that my gudesire lived on Redgauntlet's grund – they ca' the place Primrose Knowe. We had lived on the grund, and under the Redgauntlets, since the riding-days, and lang before. It was a pleasant bit; and I think the air is callerer and fresher there than onywhere else in the country. It's a' deserted now; and I sat on the broken door-cheek three days since, and was glad I couldna see the plight the place was in – but that's a' wide o' the mark. There dwelt my gudsire, Steenie Steenson; a rambling,

* A precipitous side of a mountain in Moffatdale.

rattling chiel' he had been in his young days, and could play weel on the pipes; he was famous at 'hoopers and girders,' a' Cumberland couldna touch him as 'Jockie Lattin,' and he had the finest finger for the back-lilt between Berwick and Carlisle. The like o' Steenie wasna the sort that they made Whigs o'. And so he became a Tory, as they ca' it, which we now ca' Jacobites, just out of a kind of needcessity, that he might belang to some side or other. He had nae ill-will to the Whig bodies, and liked little to see the blude rin, though, being obliged to follow Sir Robert in hunting and hoisting, watching and warding, he saw muckle mischief, and maybe did some that he couldna avoid.

Now Steenie was a kind of favourite with his master, and kenn'd a' the folk about the castle, and was often sent for to play the pipes when they were at their merriment. Auld Dougal MacCallum, the butler, that had followed Sir Robert through gude and ill, thick and thin, pool and stream, was specially fond of the pipes, and aye gae my gudesire his gude wurd wi' the laird; for Dougal could turn his master round his finger.

Weel, round came the Revolution, and it had like to hae broken the hearts baith of Dougal and his master. But the change was not a'thegither sae great as they feared and other folk thought for. The Whigs made an unco crawing what they wad do with their auld enemies, and in special wi' Sir Robert Redgauntlet. But there were ower mony great folks dipped in the same doings to make a spick-and-span new warld. So Parliament passed it a' ower easy; and Sir Robert, bating that he was held to hunting foxes instead of Covenanters, remained just the man he was. His revel was as loud, and his hall as weel lighted, as ever it had been, though maybe he lacked the fines of the Nonconformists, that used to come to stock his larder and cellar; for it is certain he began to be keener about the rents than his tenants used to find him before, and they behooved to be prompt to the rent-day or else the laird wasna pleased. And he was sic an awsome body that naebody cared to anger him; for the oaths he swore, and the rage that he used to get into, and the looks that he put on made men sometimes think him a devil incarnate.

Weel, my gudesire was nae manager – no that he was a very great misguider – but he hadna the saving gift, and he got twa terms' rent in arrear. He got the first brash at Whitsunday put ower wi' fair word and piping; but when Martinmas came there was a summons from the grund officer to come wi' the rent on a day preceese, or else Steenie behooved to flit. Sair wark he had to get the siller; but he was weel freended, and at last he got the haill scraped thegither – a thousand merks. The maist of it was from a neighbour they ca'd Laurie Lapraik – a sly tod. Laurie had wealth o' gear, could hunt wi' the hound and run wi' the hare, and be Whig or Tory, saunt or sinner, as the wind stood. He was a professor in this Revolution warld, but he liked an orra sough of this warld, and a tune on the pipes, weel aneugh at a ly-time; and, abune a', he thought he had gude security for the siller he lent my gudesireower the stocking at Primrose Knowe.

Away trots my gudesire to Redgauntlet Castle wi' a heavy purse and a light heart, glad to be out of the laird's danger. Weel, the first thing he learned at the castle was that Sir Robert had fretted himself into a fit of the gout because he did not appear before twelve o'clock. It wasna a'thegither for sake of the money, Dougal thought, but because he didna like to part wi' my gudesire aff the grund. Dougal was glad to see Steenie, and brought him into the great oak parlour; and there sat the laird his leesome lane, excepting that he had beside him a great, ill-favoured jackanape that was a special pet of his. A cankered beast it was, and mony an ill-natured trick it played; ill to please it was, and easily angered – ran about the haill castle, chattering and yowling, and pinching and biting folk, specially before ill weather, or disturbance in the state. Sir Robert ca'd it Major Weir, after the warlock that was burnt; and few folk liked either the name or the conditions of the creature – they thought there was something in it by ordinar – and my gudesire was not just easy in mind when the door shut on him, and he saw himsell in the room wi' naebody but the laird, Dougal MacCallum, and the major – a thing that hadna chanced to him before.

Sir Robert sat, or I should say, lay, in a great arm-chair, wi' his grand velvet gown, and his feet on a cradle; for he had baith gout and gravel, and his face looked as gash and ghastly as Satan's. Major Weir sat opposite to him, in a red-laced coat, and the laird's wig on his head; and aye as Sir Robert girned wi' pain, the jacka-nape girned too, like a sheep's head between a pair of tangs – an ill-faur'd, fearsome couple they were. The laird's buff-coat was hung on a pin behind him, and his broadsword and his pistols within reach; for he keepit up the auld fashion of having the weapons ready, and a horse saddled day and night, just as he used to do when he was able to loup on horseback, and sway after ony of the hill-folk he could get speerings of. Some said it was for fear of the Whigs taking vengeance, but I judge it was just his auld custom – he wasna gien to fear onything. The rental-book, wi' its black cover and brass clasps, was lying beside him; and a book of sculduddery sangs was put betwixt the leaves, to keep it open at the place where it bore evidence against the goodman of Primrose Knowe, as behind the hand with his mails and duties. Sir Robert gave my gudesire a look, as if he would have withered his heart in his bosom. Ye maun ken he had a way of bending his brows that men saw the visible mark of a horse-shoe in his forehead, deep-tinted, as if it had been stamped there.

'Are ye come light-handed, ye son of a toom whistle?' said Sir Robert. 'Zounds! if you are – '

My gudesire, with as guid a countenance as he could put on, made a leg, and placed the bag of money on the table wi' a dash, like a man that does something clever. The laird drew it to him hastily. 'Is it all here, Steenie, man?'

'Your honour will find it right,' said my gudesire.

'Here, Dougal,' said the laird, 'gie Steenie a tass of brandy till I count the siller and write out the receipt.'

But they werena weel out of the room when Sir Robert gied a yelloch that garr'd the castle rock. Back ran Dougal; in flew the liverymen; yell on yell gied the laird, ilk ane mair awfu' than the ither. My gudesire knew not whether to stand or flee, but he ventured back into the parlour, where a' was gaun hirdie-girdie – naebody to say 'come in' or 'gae out.' Terribly the laird roared for cauld water to his feet, and wine to cool his throat; and 'Hell, hell, hell, and its flames,' was aye the word in his mouth. They brought him water, and when they plunged his swoln feet into the tub, he cried out it was burning; and folks say that it *did* bubble and sparkle like a seething cauldron. He flung the cup at Dougal's head and said he had given him blood instead of Burgundy; and, sure aneugh, the lass washed clotted blood aff the carpet the neist day. The jackanape they ca'd Major Weir, it jibbered and cried as if it was mocking its master. My gudesire's head was like to turn; he forgot baith siller and receipt, and downstairs he banged; but, as he ran, the shrieks came fainter and fainter; there was a deep-drawn shivering groan, and word gaed through the castle that the laird was dead.

Weel, away came my gudesire wi' his finger in his mouth, and his best hope was that Dougal had seen the money-bag and heard the laird speak of writing the receipt. The young laird, now Sir John, came from Edinburgh to see things put to rights. Sir John and his father never 'greed weel. Sir John had been bred an advocate, and afterward sat in the last Scots Parliament and voted for the Union, having gotten, it was thought, a rug of the compensations – if his father could have come out of his grave he would have brained him

31

for it on his awn hearthstane. Some thought it was easier counting with the auld rough knight than the fair-spoken young ane – but mair of that anon.

Dougal MacCallum, poor body, neither grat nor groaned, but gaed about the house looking like a corpse, but directing, as was his duty, a' the order of the grand funeral. Now Dougal looked aye waur and waur when night was coming, and was aye the last to gang to his bed, whilk was in a little round just opposite the chamber of dais, whilk his master occupied while he was living, and where he now lay in state, as they ca'd it, weeladay! The night before the funeral Dougal could keep his awn counsel nae longer; he came doun wi' his proud spirit, and fairly asked auld Hutcheon to sit in his room with him for an hour. When they were in the round, Dougal took a tass of brandy to himsell, and gave another to Hutcheon, and wished him all health and lang life, and said that, for himsell, he wasna lang for this world; for that every night since Sir Robert's death his silver call had sounded from the state chamber just as it used to do at nights in his lifetime to call Dougal to help to turn him in his bed. Dougal said that, being alone with the dead on that floor of the tower (for naebody cared to wake Sir Robert Redgauntlet like another corpse), he had never daured to answer the call, but that now his conscience checked him for neglecting his duty; for, 'though death breaks service,' said MacCallum, 'it shall never weak my service to Sir Robert; and I will answer his next whistle, so be you will stand by me, Hutcheon.'

Hutcheon had nae will to the wark, but he had stood by Dougal in battle and broil, and he was not fail him at this pinch; so doun the carles sat ower a stoup of brandy, and Hutcheon, who was something of a clerk, would have read a chapter of the Bible; but Dougal would hear naething but a blaud of Davie Lindsay, whilk was the waur preparation.

When midnight came, and the house was quiet as the grave, sure enough the silver whistle sounded as sharp and shrill as if Sir Robert was blowing it; and up got the twa auld serving-men, and tottered into the room where the dead man lay. Hutcheon saw aneugh at the first glance; for there were torches in the room which showed him the foul fiend, in his ain shape sitting on the laird's coffin! Ower he couped as if he had been dead. He could not tell how lang he lay in a trance at the door, but when he gathered himsell he cried on his neighbour, and getting nae answer raised the house, when Dougal was found laying dead within twa steps of the bed where his master's coffin was placed. As for the whistle, it was gane anes and aye; but mony a time was it heard at the top of the house on the bartisan, and amang the auld chimneys and turrets where the howlets have their nests. Sir John hushed the matter up, and the funeral passed over without mair bogie wark.

But when a' was ower, and the laird was beginning to settle his affairs, every tenant was called up for his arrears, and my gudesir for the full sum that stood against him in the rental-book. Weel, away he trots to the castle to tell his story, and there he is introduced to Sir John, sitting in his father's chair, in deep mourning, with weepers and hanging cravat, and a small walking-rapier by his side instead of the auld broadsword that has a hundredweight of steel about it, what with blade, chape, and basket-hilt. I have heard their communings so often tauld ower that I almost think I was there mysell, though I couldna be born at the time. [In fact Alan, my companion, mimicked, with a good deal of humour, the flattering, conciliatingt one of the tenant's address and the hypocritical melancholy of the laird's reply. His grandfather, he said, had, while he spoke, his eye fixed on the rental-book as if it were a mastiff-dog that he was afraid would spring up and bite him.]

'I wuss ye joy, sir, of the head seat and the white loaf and the braid lairdship. Your father was a kind man to freends and followers; muckle grace to you, Sir John, to fill his shoon – his boots, I suld say, for he seldom wore shoon, unless it were muils when he had the gout.'

'Ay, Steenie,' quoth the laird, sighing deeply, and putting his napkin to his een 'his was a sudden call, and he will be missed in the country; no time to set his house in order – weel prepared Godward, no doubt, which is the root of the matter; but he left us behind a tangled hesp to wind, Steenie. Hem! hem! We maun go to business, Steenie; much to do, and little time to do it in.'

Here he opened the fatal volume. I have heard of a thing they call Doomsday-book – I am clear it has been a rental of backganging tenants.

'Stephen,' said Sir John, still in the same soft, sleekit tone of voice – 'Stephen Stevenson, or Steenson, ye are down here for a year's rent behind the hand – due at last term.'

Stephen. Please your honour, Sir John, I paid it to your father.

Sir John. Ye took a receipt then, doubtless, Stephen, and can produce it?

Stephen. Indeed, I hadna time, and it like your honour; for nae sooner had I set doun the siller, and just as his honour, Sir Robert, that's gaen, drew it till him to count it and write out the receipt, he was ta'en wi' the pains that removed him.

'That was unlucky,' said Sir John after a pause. 'But ye maybe paid it in the presence of somebody. I want but a *talis qualis* evidence, Stephen. I would go ower strictly to work with no poor man.'

Stephen. Troth, Sir John, there was naebody in the room but Dougal MacCallum, the butler. But, as your honour kens, he has e'en followed his auld master.

'Very unlucky again, Stephen,' said Sir John, without altering his voice a single note. 'The man to whom ye paid the money is dead, and the man who witnessed the payment is dead too; and the siller, which should have been to the fore, is neither seen nor heard tell of in the repositories. How am I to believe a' this?'

Stephen. I dinna ken, your honour; but there is a bit memorandum note of the very coins, for, God help me! I had to borrow out of twenty purses; and I am sure that ilka man there set down will take his grit oath for what purpose I borrowed the money.

Sir John. I have little doubt ye *borrowed* the money, Steenie. It is the *payment* that I want to have proof of.

Stephen. The siller maun be about the house, Sir John. And since your honour never got it, and his honour that was canna have ta'en it wi' him, maybe some of the family may hae seen it.

Sir John. We will examine the servants, Stephen; that is but reasonable.

But lackey and lass, and page and groom, all denied stoutly that they had ever seen such a bag of money as my gudesire described. What was waur, he had unluckily not mentioned to any living soul of them his purpose of paying his rent. Ae quean had noticed something under his arm, but she took it for the pipes.

Sir John Redgauntlet ordered the servants out of the room and then said to my gudesire, 'Now, Steenie, ye see ye have fair play; and, as I have little doubt ye ken better where to find the siller than ony other body, I beg in fair terms, and for your own sake, that you will end this fasherie; for, Stephen, ye maun pay or flit.'

'The Lord forgie your opinions,' said Stephen, driven almost to his wit's end; 'I am an honest man.'

'So am I, Stephen,' said his honour; 'and so are all the folks in this house, I hope. But if there be a knave among us, it must be he that tells the story he cannot prove.' He paused, and then added, mair sternly: 'If I understand your trick, sir, you want to take advantage of some malicious reports concerning things in this family, and particularly respecting my father's sudden death, thereby to cheat me out of the money, and perhaps take away my character by insinuating that I have received the rent I am demanding. Where do you suppose this money to be? I insist upon knowing.'

My gudesire saw everything look sae muckle against him that he grew nearly desperate. However, he shifted from one foot to another, looked to every corner of the room, and made no answer.

'Speak out, sirrah,' said the laird, assuming a look of his father's, a very particular ane, which he had when he was angry – it seemed as if the wrinkles of his frown made that selfsame fearful shape of a horse's shoe in the middle of his brow; 'speak out, sir! I *will* know your thoughts; do you suppose that I have this money?'

'Far be it frae me to say so,' said Stephen.

'Do you charge any of my people with having taken it?'

'I wad be laith to charge them that may be innocent,' said my gudesire; 'and if there be any one that is guilty, I have nae proof.'

'Somewhere the money must be, if there is a word of truth in your story,' said Sir John; 'I ask where you think it is – and demand a correct answer!'

'In hell, if you *will* have my thoughts of it,' said my gudesire, driven to extremity – 'in hell! with your father, his jackanape, and his silver whistle.'

Down the stairs he ran (for the parlour was nae place for him after such a word), and he heard the laird swearing blood and wounds behind him as fast as ever did Sir Robert, and roaring for the bailie and the baron-officer.

Away rode my gudesire to his chief creditor (him they ca'd Laurie Lapraik), to try if he could make onything out of him; but when he tauld his story, he got but the worst word in his wame – thief, beggar, and dyvour were the saftest terms; and to the boot of these hard terms Laurie brought up the auld story of dipping his hand in the blood of God's saunts, just as if a tenant could have helped riding with the laird, and that a laird like Sir Robert Redgauntlet. My gudesire was, by this time, far beyond the bounds of patience, and, while he and Laurie were at deil speed the liars, he was wanchancie aneugh to abuse Lapraik's doctrine as weel as the man, and said things that garr'd folks' flesh grue that heard them – he wasna just himsell, and he had lived wi' a wild set in his day.

At last they parted, and my gudesire was to ride hame through the wood of Pitmurkie, that is a' fou of black firs, as they say. I ken the wood, but the firs may be black or white for what I can tell. At the entry of the wood there is a wild common, and on the edge of the common a little lonely change-house that was keepit then by a hostler wife – they suld hae ca'd her Tibbie Faw – and there puir Steenie cried for a mutchkin of brandy, for he had had no refreshment the haill day. Tibbie was earnest wi' him to take a bite of meat, but he couldna think o' 't, nor would he take his foot out of the stirrup, and took off the brandy wholely at twa draughts, and named a toast at each. The first was, the memory of Sir Robert Redgauntlet, and may he never lie quiet in his grave till he had righted his poor bond-tenant; and the second was, a health to Man's Enemy, if he would but get him back the pock of siller or tell him what came o' 't, for he saw the haill world was like to regard him as a thief and a cheat, and he took that waur than even the ruin of his house and hauld.

On he rode, little caring where. It was a dark night turned and the trees made it yet darker, and he let the beast take its ain road through the wood; when all of a sudden, from tired and wearied that it was before, the nag began to spring and flee and stend, that my gudesire could hardly keep the saddle. Upon the whilk, a horseman, suddenly riding up beside him, said, 'That's a mettle beast of yours, freend; will you sell him?' So saying, he touched the horse's neck with his riding-wand, and it fell into its auld heigh-ho of stumbling a trot. 'But his spunk's soon out of him, I think,' continued the stranger, 'and that is like mony a man's courage, that thinks he wad do great things.'

My gudesire scarce listened to this, but spurred his horse, with, 'Gude-e'en to you, freend.'

But it's like the stranger was ane that doesna lightly yield his point; for, ride as Steenie liked, he was aye beside him at the self-same pace. At last my gudesire, Steenie Steenson, grew half angry and, to say the truth, half feard.

'What is that you want with me, freend?' he said. 'If ye be a robber, I have nae money; if ye be a leal man, wanting company, I have nae heart to mirth or speaking; and if ye want to ken the road, I scarce ken it mysell.'

'If you will tell me your grief,' said the stranger, 'I am one that, though I have been sair misca'd in the world, am the only hand for helping my freends.'

So my gudesire, to ease his ain heart mair than from any hope of help, told him the story from beginning to end.

'It's a hard pinch,' said the stranger; 'but I think I can help you.'

'If you could lend the money, sir, and take a lang day – I ken nae other help on earth,' said my gudesire.

'But there may be some under the earth,' said the stranger. 'Come, I'll be frank wi' you; I could lend you the money on bond, but you would maybe scruple my terms. Now I can tell you that your auld laird is disturbed in his grave by your curses and the wailing of your family, and if ye daur venture to go to see him he will give you the receipt.'

My gudesire's hair stood on end at this proposal, but he thought his companion might be some humoursome chield that was trying to frighten him, and might end with lending him the money. Besides, he was bauld wi' brandy and desperate wi' distress; and he said he had courage to go to the gate of hell, and a step farther, for that receipt. The stranger laughed.

Weel, they rode on through the thickest of the wood, when, all of a sudden, the horse stopped at the door of a great house; and, but that he knew the place was ten miles off, my father would have thought he was at Redgauntlet Castle. They rode into the outer courtyard, through the muckle faulding yetts, and aneath the auld portcullis; and the whole front of the house was lighted, and there were pipes and fiddles, and as much dancing and deray within as used to be at Sir Robert's house at Pace and Yule, and such high seasons. They lap off, and my gudesire, as seemed to him, fastened his horse to the very ring he had tied him to that morning when he gaed to wait on the young Sir John.

'God!' said my gudesire, 'if Sir Robert's death be but a dream!'

He knocked at the ha' door just as he was wont, and his auld acquaintance, Dougal MacCallum – just after his wont, too – came to open the door, and said, 'Piper Steenie, are ye there, lad? Sir Robert has been crying for you.'

My gudesire was like a man in a dream; he looked for the stranger, but he was gane for the time. At last he just tried to say, 'Ha! Dougal Driveower, are you living? I thought ye had been dead.'

'Never fash yoursell wi' me,' said Dougal, 'but look to yoursell; and see ye tak' naething frae onybody here, neither meat, drink, or siller, except the receipt that is your ain.'

So saying, he led the way out through halls and trances that were weel kenn'd to my gudesire, and into the auld oak parlour; and there was as much singing of profane sangs, and birling of red wine, and blasphemy and sculduddery as had ever been in Redgauntlet Castle when it was at the blythest.

But Lord take us in keeping! what a set of ghastly revellers there were that sat around that table! My gudesire kenn'd mony that had long before gane to their place, for often had he piped to the most part in the hall of Redgauntlet. There was the fierce Middleton, and the dissolute Rothes, and the crafty Lauderdale; and Dalyell, with his bald head and a beard to his girdle; and Earlshall, with Cameron's blude on his hand; and wild Bonshaw, that tied blessed Mr Cargill's limbs till the blude sprung; and Dumbarton Douglas, the twice-turned traitor baith to country and king. There was the Bluidy Advocate MacKenyie, who, for his wordly wit and wisdom, had been to the rest as a god. And there was Claverhouse, as beautiful as when he lived, with his long, dark curled locks streaming down over his laced buff-coat, and with his left hand always on his right spule-blade, to hide the wound that the silver bullet had made. He sat apart from them all, and looked at them with a melancholy, haughty countenance; while the rest hallooed and sang and laughed, that the room rang. But their smiles were fearfully contorted from time to time; and their laughter passed into such wild sounds as made my gudesire's very nails grow blue, and chilled the marrow in his banes.

They that waited at the table were just the wicked serving-men and troopers that had done their work and cruel bidding on earth. There was the Lang Lad of the Nethertown, that helped to take Argyle; and the bishop's summoner, that they called the Deil's Rattlebag; and the wicked guardsmen in their laced coats; and the savage Highland Amorites, that shed blood like water; and mony a proud serving-man, haughty of heart and bloody of hand, cringing to the rich and making them wickeder than they would be, grinding the poor to powder when the rich had broken them to fragments. And mony, mony mair were coming and ganging, a' as busy in their vocation as if they had been alive.

Sir Robert Redgauntlet, in the midst of a' this fearful riot, cried, wi' a voice like thunder, on Steenie Piper to come to the board-head where he was sitting, his legs stretched out before him and swathed up with flannel, with his holster pistols aside him, while the great broadsword rested against his chair, just as my gudesire had seen him the last time upon earth; the very cushion for the jackanape was close to him, but the creature itsell was not there – it wasna its hour, it's likely; for he heard them say, as he came forward. 'Is not the major come yet?' And another answered, 'The Jackanape will be here betimes the morn.' And when my gudesire came forward, Sir Robert, or his ghaist, or the deevil in his likeness, said, 'Weel, piper, hae ye settled wi' my son for the year's rent?'

With much ado my father gat breath to say that Sir John would not settle without his honour's receipt.

'Ye shall hae that for a tune of the pipes, Steenie,' said the appearance of Sir Robert; 'play us up "Weel Hoddled, Luckie." '

Now this was a tune my gudesire learned frae a warlock, that heard it when they were worshipping Satan at their meetings; and my gudesire had sometimes played it at the ranting suppers in

Redgauntlet Castle, but never very willingly; and now he grew cauld at the very name of it, and said, for excuse, he hadna his pipes wi' him.

'MacCallum, ye limb of Beelzebub,' said the fearfu' Sir Robert, 'bring Steenie the pipes that I am keeping for him!'

MacCallum brought a pair of pipes might have served the piper of Donald of the Isles. But he gave my gudesire a nudge as he offered them; and looking secretly and closely, Steenie saw that the chanter was of steel, and heated to a white heat; so he had fair warning not to trust his fingers with it. So he excused himsell again, and said he was faint and frightened, and had not wind aneugh to fill the bag.

'Then ye maun eat and drink, Steenie,' said the figure, 'for we do little else here, and it's ill speaking between a fou man and a fasting.'

Now these were the very words that the bloody Earl of Douglas said to keep the king's messenger in hand while he cut the head off MacLellan of Bombie, at the Threave Castle; and that put Steenie mair and mair on his guard. So he spoke up like a man, and said he came neither to eat nor drink nor make minstrelsy, but simply for his ain – to ken what was come o' the money he had paid, and to get a discharge for it; and he was so stout-hearted by this time that he charged Sir Robert for conscience' sake (he had no power to say the holy name), and as he hoped for peace and rest, to spread no snares for him, but just to give him his ain.

The appearance gnashed its teeth and laughed, but it took from a large pocket-book the receipt, and handed it to Steenie. 'There is your receipt, ye pitiful cur; and for the money, my dog-whelp of a son may go look for it in the Cat's Cradle.'

My gudesire uttered mony thanks, and was about to retire, when Sir Robert roared aloud: 'Stop, though, thou sack-doudling son of a – ! I am not done with thee. HERE we do nothing for nothing; and you must return on this very day twelvemonth to pay your master the homage that you owe me for my protection.'

My father's tongue was loosed of a suddenty, and he said aloud. 'I refer myself to God's pleasure, and not to yours.'

He had no sooner uttered the word than all was dark around him; and he sank on the earth with such a sudden shock that he lost both breath and sense.

How lang Steenie lay there he could not tell; but when he came to himsell he was lying in the auld kirkyard of Redgauntlet parochine, just at the door of the family aisle, and the scutcheon of the auld knight, Sir Robert, hanging over his head. There was a deep morning fog on grass and gravestane around him, and his horse was feeding quietly beside the minister's twa cows. Steenie would have thought the whole was a dream, but he had the receipt in his hand fairly written and signed by the auld laird; only the last letters of his name were a little disorderly, written like one seized with sudden pain.

Sorely troubled in his mind, he left that dreary place, rode through the mist to Redgauntlet Castle, and with much ado he got speech of the laird.

'Well, you dyvour bankrupt,' was the first word, 'have you brought me my rent?'

'No,' answered my gudesire. 'I have not; but I have brought your honour Sir Robert's receipt for it.'

'How, sirrah? Sir Robert's receipt! You told me he had not given you one.'

'Will your honour please to see if that bit line is right?'

Sir John looked at every line, and at every letter, with much attention; and at last at the date, which my gudesire had not observed – 'From my appointed place,' he read, 'this twenty-fifth of November.'

'What! That is yesterday! Villain, thou must have gone to hell for this!'

'I got it from your honour's father; whether be he in heaven or hell, I know not,' said Steenie.

'I will debate you for a warlock to the Privy Council!' said Sir John. 'I will send you to your master, the devil, with the help of a tar-barrel and a torch!'

'I intend to debate mysell to the Presbytery,' said Steenie 'and tell them all I have seen last night, whilk are things fitter for them to judge of than a borrel man like me.'

Sir John paused, composed himself, and desired to hear the full history; and my gudesire told it him from point to point, as I have told it you – neither more nor less.

Sir John was silent again for a long time, and at last he said very composedly: 'Steenie, this story of yours concerns the honour of many a noble family besides mine; and if it be a leasing-making, to keep yourself out of my danger, the least you can expect is to have a red-hot iron driven through your tongue, and that will be as bad as scauding your fingers wi' a red-hot chanter. But yet it may be true, Steenie, and if the money cast up I shall not know what to think of it. But where shall we find the Cat's Cradle? There are cats enough about the old house, but I think they kitten without the ceremony of bed or cradle.'

'We were best ask Hutcheon,' said my gudesire; 'he kens a' the odd corners about as weel as – another serving-man that is no gane, and that I wad not like to name.'

Aweel, Hutcheon, when he was asked, told them that a ruinous turret lang disused, next to the clock-house, only accessible by a ladder, for the opening was on the outside, above the battlements, was called of old the Cat's Cradle.

'There will I go immediately,' said Sir John; and he took with what purpose Heaven kens – one of his father's pistols from the hall-table, where they had lain since the night he died, and hastened to the battlements.

It was a dangerous place to climb, for the ladder was auld and frail, and wanted ane or twa rounds. However, up got Sir John, and entered at the turret door, where his body stopped the only little light that was in the bit turret. Something flees at him wi' a vengeance, maist dang him back ower – bang! gaed the knight's pistol, and Hutcheon, that held the ladder, and my gudesire, that stood beside him, hears a loud skelloch. A minute after, Sir John flings the body of the jackanape down to them, and cries that the siller is fund and that they should come up and help him. And there was the bag of siller sure aneugh, and mony orra thing besides that had been missing for mony a day. And Sir John, when he had riped the turret weel, led my gudesire into the dining-parlour, and took him by the hand, and spoke kindly to him, and said he was sorry he should have doubted his word, and that he would here-after be a good master to him, to make amends.

'And now, Steenie,' said Sir John, 'although this vision of yours tends, on the whole, to my father's credit as an honest man, that he should, even after his death, desire to see justice done to a poor man like you, yet you are sensible that ill-dispositioned men might make bad constructions upon it concerning his soul's health. So, I think, we had better lay the haill dirdum on that ill-deedie creature, Major Weir, and say naething about your dream in the wood of Pitmurkie. You had ta'en ower muckle brandy to be very certain about onything; and, Steenie, this receipt' – his hand shook while he held it out – ' it's but a queer kind of document, and we will do best. I think, to put it quietly in the fire.'

'Od, but for as queer as it is, it's a' the voucher I have for my rent,' said my gudesire, who was afraid, it may be, of losing the benefit of Sir Robert's discharge.

'I will bear the contents to your credit in the rental-book, and give you a discharge under my own hand,' said Sir John, 'and that on the spot. And, Steenie, if you can hold your tongue about this

41

matter, you shall sit, from this time downward, at an easier rent.'

'Mony thanks to your honour,' said Steenie, who saw easily in what corner the wind was; 'doubtless I will be conformable to all your honour's commands; only I would willingly speak wi' some power minister on the subject, for I do not like the sort of soumons of appointment whilk your honour's father – '

'Do not call the phantom my father!' said Sir John, interrupting him.

'Well, then, the thing that was so like him,' said my gudesire; 'he spoke of my coming back to see him this time twelvemonth, and it's a weight on my conscience.'

'Aweel, then,' said Sir John, 'if you be so much distressed in mind, you may speak to our minister of the parish; he is a douce man, regards the honour of our family, and the mair that he may look for some patronage from me.'

Wi' that, my father readily agreed that the receipt should be burned; and the laird threw it into the chimney with his ain hand. Burn it would not for them, though; but away it flew up the lum, wi' a long train of sparks at its tail, and a hissing noise like a squib.

My gudesire gaed down to the manse, and the minister, when he had heard the story, said it was his real opinion that, though my gudesire had gaen very far in tampering with dangerous matters, yet as he had refused the devil's arles (for such was the offer of meat and drink), and had refused to do homage by piping at his bidding, he hoped that, if he held a circumspect walk hereafter, Satan could take little advantage by what was come and gane. And, indeed, my gudesire, of his ain accord, lang forswore baith the pipes and the brandy – it was not even till the year was out, and the fatal day past, that he would so much as take the fiddle or drink usquebaugh or tippenny.

Sir John made up his story about the jackanape as he liked himsell; and some believe till this day there was no more in the matter than the filching nature of the brute. Indeed, ye'll no hinder some to threap that it was nane o' the auld Enemy that Dougal and Hutcheon saw in the laird's room, but only that wanchancie creature the major, capering on the coffin; and that, as to the blawing on the laird's whistle that was heard after he was dead, the filthy brute could do that as weel as the laird himself, if not better. But Heaven kens the truth, whilk first came out by the minister's wife, after Sir John and her ain gudeman were baith in the moulds. And then my gudesire, wha was failed in his limbs, but not in his judgement or memory – at least nothing to speak of – was obliged to tell the real narrative to his friends, for the credit of his good name. He might else have been charged for a warlock.

The shades of evening were growing thicker around us as my conductor finished his long narrative with this moral: 'You see, birkie, it is nae chancy thing to tak' a stranger traveller for a guide when you are in an uncouth land.'

'I should not have made that inference,' said I. 'Your grandfather's adventure was fortunate for himself, whom it saved from ruin and distress, and fortunate for his landlord.'

"Ay, but they had baith to sup the sauce o' 't sooner or later,' said Wandering Willie; 'what was fristed wasna forgiven. Sir John died before he was much over threescore, and it was just like of a moment's illness. And for my gudesire, though he departed in fulness of life, yet there was my father, a yauld man of forty-five, fell down betwixt the stilts of his plough, and rase never again, and left naie bairn but me – a puir, sightless, fatherless, motherless creature, could neither work nor want. Things gaed well aneugh at first, for Sir Regwald Redgauntlet, the only son of Sir John and the oye of auld Sir Robert, and, wae's me! the last of the honourable house, took the farm aff our hands and brought me into his household to have care of me. My head never settled since I lost him; and if I say another word about it, deil a bar will I have the heart to play the night. Look out, my gentle chap,' he resumed, in a different tone; 'ye should see the lights at Brokenburn Glen by this time.'

THE WOW O' RIVVEN

ELSIE SCOTT had let her work fall on her knees, and her hands on her work, and was looking out of the wide, low window of her room, which was on one of the ground-floors of the village street. Through a gap in the household shrubbery of fuchsias and myrtles filling the window-sill, one passing on the foot-pavement might get a momentary glimpse of her pale face, lighted up with two blue eyes, over which some inward trouble had spread a faint, gauze-like haziness. But almost before her thoughts had had time to wander back to this trouble, a shout of children's voices, at the other end of the street, reached her ear. She listened a moment. A shadow of displeasure and pain crossed her countenance; and rising hastily, she betook herself to an inner apartment, and closed the door behind her.

Meantime the sounds drew nearer; and by-and-by an old man, whose strange appearance and dress showed that he had little capacity either for good or evil, passed the window. His clothes were comfortable enough in quality and condition, for they were the annual gift of a benevolent lady in the neighbourhood; but, being made to accommodate his taste, both known and traditional, they were somewhat peculiar in cut and adornment.

Both coat and trousers were of a dark grey cloth; but the former, which in its shape partook of the military, had a straight collar of yellow, and narrow cuffs of the same; while upon both sleeves, about the place where a corporal wears his stripes, was expressed, in the same yellow cloth, a somewhat singular device. It was as close an imitation of a bell, with its tongue hanging out of its mouth, as the tailor's skill could produce from a single piece of cloth. The origin of the military cut of his coat was well known. His preference for it arose in the time of the wars of the first Napoleon, when the threatened invasion of the country caused the organisation of many volunteer regiments.

The martial show and exercises captivated the poor man's fancy; and from that time forward nothing pleased his vanity, and consequently conciliated his good-will more, than to style him by his favourite title – the *Colonel*. But the badge on his arm had a deeper origin, which will be partially manifest in the course of the story – if story it can be called. It was, indeed, the course of the fool, the outward and visible sign of his relation to the infinite and unseen. His countenance, however, although the features were not of any peculiarly low or animal type, showed no corresponding sign of the consciousness of such a relation, being as vacant as human countenance could well be.

The cause of Elsie's annoyance was that the fool was annoyed; he was followed by a troop of boys, who turned his rank into scorn, and assailed him with epithets hateful to him. Although the most harmless of creatures when let alone, he was dangerous when roused; and now he stooped repeatedly to pick up stones and hurl them at his tormentors, who took care, while abusing him, to keep at a considerable distance, lest he should get hold of them.

Amidst the sounds of derision that followed him, might be heard the words frequently repeated – '*Come hame, come hame.*' But in a few minutes the noise ceased, either from the interference of some friendly inhabitant, or that the boys grew weary, and departed in search of other amusement. By-and-by Elsie might be seen again at her work in the window; but the cloud over her eyes was deeper, and her whole face more sad.

Indeed, so much did the persecution of this poor man affect her, that an onlooker would have been compelled to seek the cause in some yet deeper sympathy than that commonly felt for the oppressed, even by women. And such a sympathy existed, strange as it may seem, between the beautiful girl (for many called her a *bonnie lassie*) and this 'tatter of humanity.' Nothing would have been farther from the thoughts of those that knew them, than the supposition of any correspondence or connection between them; yet this sympathy sprang in part from a real similarity in their history and present condition.

All the facts that were known about *Feel Jock's* origin were these: that seventy years ago, a man who had gone with his horse and cart some miles from the village, to fetch home a load of peat from a desolate *moss*, had heard, while toiling along as rough a road on as lonely a hillside as any in Scotland, the cry of a child; and, searching about, had found the infant, hardly wrapped in rags, and untended, as if the earth herself had just given him birth – that desert moor, wide and dismal, broken and watery, the only bosom for him to lie upon, and the cold, clear night-heaven his only covering. The man had brought him home, and the parish had taken parish-care of him.

He had grown up, and proved what he now was – almost an idiot. Many of the townspeople were kind to him, and employed him in fetching water for them from the river or wells in the neighbourhood, paying him for his trouble in victuals, or whisky, of which he was very fond. He seldom spoke; and the sentences he could utter were few; yet the tone, and even the words of his limited vocabulary were sufficient to express gratitude, and some measure of love towards those who were kind to him, and hatred of those who teased and insulted him. He lived a life without aim, and apparently to no purpose; in this resembling most of his more gifted fellow-men, who, with all the tools and materials necessary for building a noble mansion, are yet content with a clay hut.

Elsie, on the contrary, had been born in a comfortable farm-house, amidst homeliness and abundance. But at a very early age she had lost both father and mother; not so early, however, but that she had faint memories of warm soft times on her mother's bosom, and of refuge in her mother's arms from the attacks of geese, and the pursuit of pigs. Therefore, in after-times, when she looked forward to heaven, it was as much a reverting to the old heavenly times of childhood and mother's love, as an anticipation of something yet to be revealed.

Indeed, without some such memory, how should we ever picture to ourselves a perfect rest? But sometimes it would seem as if the more a heart was made capable of loving, the less it had to love; and poor Elsie, in passing from a mother's to a brother's guardian-ship, felt a change of spiritual temperature too keen. He was not a bad man, or incapable of benevolence when touched by the sight of want in anything of which he would himself have felt the privation; but he was so coarsely made, that only the purest animal necessities affected him, and a hard word, or unfeeling speech, could never have reached the quick of his nature, through the hide that enclosed it. Elsie, on the contrary, was excessively and painfully sensitive, as if her nature constantly portended an invisible multitude of half-spiritual, half-nervous antennae, which shrank and trembled in every current of air at all below their own temperature.

The effect of this upon her behaviour was such that she was called odd; and the poor girl felt she was not like other people, yet could not help it. Her brother, too, laughed at her without the slightest idea of the pain he occasioned, or the remotest feeling of curiosity as to what the inward and consistent causes of the outward ab-normal condition might be. Tenderness was the divine comforting she needed; and it was altogether absent from her brother's character and behaviour.

Her neighbours looked on her with some interest, but they rather shunned than courted her acquaintance; especially after the return of certain nervous attacks to which she had been subject in childhood, and which were again brought on by the events I must relate. It is curious how certain diseases repel, by a kind of awe, the sympathies of the neighbours: as if, by the fact of being subject to them, the patient were removed into another realm of existence from which, like the dead with the living, she can hold communion with those around her only partially, and with a mixture of dread pervading the intercourse.

Thus some of the deepest, purest wells of spiritual life, are, like those in old castles, choked up by the decay of the outer walls. But what tended more than anything, perhaps, to keep up the painful unrest of her soul (for the beauty of her character was evident in the fact, that the irritation seldom reached her *mind*), was a circumstance at which, in its present connection, some of my readers will smile, and others feel a shudder corresponding in kind to that of Elsie.

Her brother was very fond of a rather small, but ferocious-looking bull-dog, which followed close at his heels, wherever he went, with hanging head and slouching gait, never leaping or racing about like other dogs. When in the house, he always lay under his master's chair. He seemed to dislike Elsie, and she felt an unspeakable repugnance to him.

Though she never mentioned her aversion, her brother easily saw it by the way in which she avoided the animal; and attributing it entirely to fear – which indeed had a great share in the matter – he would cruelly aggravate it, by telling her stories of the fierce hardihood and relentless persistency of this kind of animal. He dared not yet further increase her terror by offering to set the creature upon her, because it was doubtful whether he might be able to restrain him; but the mental suffering which he occasioned by this heartless conduct, and for which he had no sympathy, was as severe as many bodily sufferings to which he would have been sorry to subject her. Whenever the poor girl happened inadvertently to pass near the dog, which was seldom, a low growl made her aware of his proximity, and drove her to a quick retreat. He was, in fact, the animal impersonation of the animal opposition which she had continually to endure. Like chooses like; and the bull-dog *in* her brother made choice of the bull-dog *out* of him for his companion. So her day was one of shrinking fear and multiform discomfort.

But a nature capable of so much distress must of necessity be *capable* of a corresponding amount of pleasure; and in her case this was manifest in the fact, that sleep and the quiet of her own room restored her wonderfully. If she was only let alone, a calm mood, filled with images of pleasure, soon took possession of her mind.

Her acquaintance with the fool had commenced some ten years previous to the time I write of, when she was quite a little girl, and had come from the country with her brother, who, having taken a small farm close to the town, preferred residing in the town to occupying the farm-house, which was not comfortable. She looked at first with some terror on his uncouth appearance, and with much wonderment on his strange dress.

This wonder was heightened by a conversation she overheard one day in the street between the fool and a little pale-faced boy, who, approaching him respectfully, said, 'Weel, cornel!'

'Weel, laddie!' was the reply.

'Fat dis the wow say, cornel?'

'Come hame, come hame!' answered the *colonel*, with both accent and quantity heaped on the word *hame*.

What the *wow* could be, she had no idea; only, as the years passed on, the strange word became in her mind indescribably associated with the strange shape in yellow cloth on his sleeves. Had she been a native of the town, she could not have failed to know its import, so familiar was every one with it, although it did not belong to the local vocabulary; but, as it was, years passed away before she discovered its meaning. And when, again and again, the fool, attempting to convey his gratitude for some kindness she had shown him, mumbled over the words – '*The wow o' Rivven – the wow o' Rivven*,' the wonder would return as to what could be the idea associated with them in his mind, but she made no advance towards their explanation.

That, however, which most attracted her to the old man, was his persecution by the children. They were to him what the bulldog was to her – the constant source of irritation and annoyance. They could hardly hurt him, nor did he appear to dread other injury from them than insult, to which, fool though he was, he was keenly alive. Human gad-flies that they were! they sometimes stung him beyond endurance, and he would curse them in the impotence of his anger.

Once or twice Elsie had been so far carried beyond her constitutional timidity, by sympathy for the distress of her friend, that she had gone out and talked to the boys, – even scolded them, so that they slunk away ashamed, and began to stand as much in dread of her as of the clutches of their prey. So she, gentle and timid to excess, acquired among them the reputation of a termagant. Popular opinion among children, as among men, is often just, but as often very unjust; for the same manifestations may proceed from opposite principles; and, therefore, as indices to character, may mislead as often as enlighten.

Next door to the house in which Elsie resided, dwelt a tradesman and his wife, who kept an indefinite sort of shop in which various kinds of goods were exposed for sale. Their youngest son was about the same age as Elsie; and while they were rather more than children, and less than young people, he spent many of his evenings with her, somewhat to the loss of position in his classes at the parish school. They were, indeed, much attached to each other; and, peculiarly constituted as Elsie was, one may imagine what kind of heavenly messenger a companion stronger than herself must have been to her.

In fact, if she could have framed the undefinable need of her child-like nature into an articulate prayer, it would have been – 'Give me some one to love me stronger than I.'

Any love was helpful, yes, in its degree saving to her poor troubled soul; but the hope, as they grew older together, that the powerful, yet tender-hearted youth, really loved her, and would one day make her his wife, was like the opening of heavenly eyes of life and love in the hitherto blank and deathlike face of her existence. But nothing had been said of love, although they met and parted like lovers.

Doubtless, if the circles of their thought and feeling had continued as now to intersect each other, there would have been no interruption to their affection; but the time at length arrived when the old couple, seeing the rest of their family comfortably settled in life, resolved to make a gentleman of the youngest; and so sent him from school to college. The facilities existing in Scotland for providing a professional training enabled them to educate him as a surgeon. He parted from Elsie with some regret; but, far less dependent on her than she was on him, and full of the prospects of the future, he felt none of that sinking at the heart which seemed to lay her whole nature open to a fresh inroad of all the terrors and sorrows of her peculiar existence. No correspondence took place between them. New pursuits and relations and the development of his tastes and judgements, entirely altered the position of poor Elsie in his memory.

Having been, during their intercourse, far less of a man than she of a woman, he had no definite idea of the place he had occupied

49

in her regard; and in his mind she receded into the background of the past, without his having any idea that she would suffer thereby, or that he was unjust towards her; while, in her thoughts, his image stood in the highest and clearest relief. It was the centre-point from which and towards which all lines radiated and converged, and although she could not but be doubtful about the future, yet there was much hope mingled with her doubts.

But when, at the close of two years, he visited his native village, and she saw before her, instead of the homely youth who had left her that winter evening, one who, to her inexperienced eyes, appeared a finished gentleman, her heart sank within her, as if she had found Nature herself false in her ripening processes, destroying the beautiful promise of a former year by changing instead of developing her creations. He spoke kindly to her, but not cordially. To her ear the voice seemed to come from a great distance out of the past; and while she looked upon him, that optical change passed over her vision which all have experienced after gazing abstractedly on any object for a time: his form grew very small, and receded to an immeasurable distance; till, her imagination mingling with the twilight haze of her senses, she seemed to see him standing far off on a hill, with the bright horizon of sunset for a background to his clearly-defined figure.

She knew no more till she found herself in bed in the dark; and the first message that reached her from the outward world was the infernal growl of the bull-dog from the room below. Next day she saw her lover walking with two ladies, who would have thought it some degree of condescension to speak to her; and he passed the house without once looking towards it.

One who is sufficiently possessed by the demon of nervousness to be glad of the magnetic influences of a friend's company in a public promenade, or of a horse beneath him in passing through a churchyard, will have some faint idea of how utterly exposed and defenceless poor Elsie now felt on the crowded thoroughfare of life.

And so the insensibility which had overtaken her was not the ordinary swoon with which nature relieves the overstrained nerves, but the return of the epileptic fits of her early childhood; and if the condition of the poor girl had been pitiable before, it was tenfold more so now. Yet she did not complain, but bore all in silence, though it was evident that her health was giving way. But now, help came to her from a strange quarter; though many might not be willing to accord the name of help to that which rather hastened than retarded the progress of her decline.

She had gone to spend a few of the summer days with a relative in the country, some miles from her home, if home it could be called. One evening, towards sunset, she went out for a solitary walk. Passing from the little garden gate, she went along a bare country road for some distance, and then, turning aside by a foot-path through a thicket of low trees, she came out in a lonely little churchyard on the hillside.

Hardly knowing whether or not she had intended to go there, she seated herself on a mound covered with long grass, one of many. Before her stood the ruins of an old church, which was taking centuries to crumble. Little remained but the gable-wall, immensely thick, and covered with ancient ivy. The rays of the setting sun fell on a mound at its foot, not green like the rest, but of a rich red-brown in the rosy sunset, and evidently but newly heaped up. Her eyes, too, rested upon it. Slowly the sun sank below the near horizon.

As the last brilliant point disappeared, the ivy darkened, and a wind arose and shook all its leaves, making them look cold and troubled; and to Elsie's ear came a low faint sound, as from a far-off bell. But close beside her – and she started and shivered at the sound – rose a deep, monotonous, almost, sepulchral voice, *'Come hame, come hame! The wow, the wow!'*

At once she understood the whole. She sat in the churchyard of the ancient parish church of Ruthven; and when she lifted up her eyes, there she saw, in the half-ruined belfry, the old bell, all but hidden with ivy, which the passing wind had roused to utter one sleepy tone; and there, beside her, stood the fool with the bell on his arm, and to him and to her the *wow o' Rivven* said, *'Come hame, come hame!'*

Ah, what did she want in the whole universe of God but a home? And though the ground beneath was hard, and the sky overhead far and boundless, and the hillside lonely and companionless, yet somewhere within the visible, and beyond these the outer surfaces of creation, there might be a home for her; as round the wintry house the snows lie heaped up cold and white and dreary all the long *forenight*, while within, beyond the closed shutters, and giving no glimmer through the thick stone walls, the fires are blazing joyously and the voices and laughter of young unfrozen children are heard, and nothing belongs to winter but the grey hairs on the heads of the parents, within whose warm hearts child-like voices are heard, and child-like thoughts move to and fro. The kernel of winter itself is spring, or a sleeping summer.

It was no wonder that the fool, cast out of the earth on a far more desolate spot than this, should seek to return within her bosom at this place of open doors, and should call it *home*. For surely the surface of the earth had no home for him. The mound at the foot of the gable contained the body of one who had shown him kindness. He had followed the funeral that afternoon from the town, and had remained behind with the bell. Indeed it was his custom, though Elsie had not known it, to follow every funeral going to this, his favourite church-yard of Ruthven; and, possibly in imitation of its booming, for it was still tolled at the funeral, she had given the old bell the name of *the wow*, and had translated its monotonous clangour into the articulate sounds – *come hame, come hame*.

What precise meaning he attached to the words it is impossible to say; but it was evident that the place possessed a strange attraction for him, drawing him towards it by the cords of some spiritual magnetism. It is possible that in the mind of the idiot there may have been some feeling about this church yard and bell, which, in the mind of another, would have become a grand poetic thought; a feeling as if the ghostly old bell hung at the church-door of the invisible world, and ever and anon rung out joyous notes (though they sounded sad in the ears of the living), calling to the children of the unseen to *come home, come home*. She sat for some time in silence; for the bell did not ring again, and the fool spoke no more; till the dews began to fall, when she rose and went home, followed by her companion, who passed the night in the barn.

From that hour Elsie was furnished with a visual image of the rest she sought; an image which, mingling with deeper and holier thoughts, became, like the bow set in the cloud, the earthly pledge and sign of the fulfilment of heavenly hopes. Often when the wintry fog of cold discomfort and homelessness filled her soul, all at once the picture of the little churchyard – with the old gable and belfry, and the slanting sunlight steeping down to the very roots of the long grass on the graves – arose in the darkened chamber (*camera obscura*) of her soul; and again she heard the faint Æolian sound of the bell, and the voice of the prophet-fool who interpreted the oracle; and the inward weariness was soothed by the promise of a long sleep.

Who can tell how many have been counted fools simply because they were prophets; or how much of the madness in the world may be the utterance of thoughts true and just, but belonging to a region differing from ours in its nature and scenery!

But to Elsie looking out of her window came the mocking tones of the idle boys who had chosen as the vehicle of their scorn the very words which showed the relation of the fool to the eternal, and revealed in him an element higher far than any yet developed in them. They turned his glory into shame, like the enemies of David when they mocked the would-be king. And the best in a man is often that which is most condemned by those who have not attained to his goodness. The words, however, even as repeated by the boys, had not solely awakened indignation at the persecution of the old man: they had likewise comforted her with the thought of the refuge that awaited both him and her.

But the same evening a worse trial was in store for her. Again she sat near the window, oppressed by the consciousness that her brother had come in. He had gone upstairs, and his dog had remained at the door, exchanging surly compliments with some of his own kind, when the fool came strolling past, and, I do not know from what cause, the dog flew at him. Elsie heard his cry and looked up. Her fear of the brute vanished in a moment before her sympathy for her friend. She darted from the house, and rushed towards the dog to drag him off the defenceless idiot, calling him by his name in a tone of anger and dislike. He left the fool, and, springing at Elsie, seized her by the arm above the elbow with such a grip that, in the midst of her agony, she fancied she heard the bone crack. But she uttered no cry, for the most apprehensive are sometimes the most courageous.

Just then, however, her former lover was coming along the street, and, catching a glimpse of what had happened, was on the spot in an instant, took the dog by the throat with a grip not inferior to his own, and having thus compelled him to relax his hold, dashed him on the ground with a force that almost stunned him, and then with a super-added kick sent him away limping and howling; whereupon the fool, attacking him furiously with a stick, would certainly have finished him, had not his master descried his plight and come to his rescue.

Meantime the young surgeon had carried Elsie into the house; for, as soon as she was rescued from the dog, she had fallen down in one of her fits, which were becoming more and more frequent of themselves, and little needed such a shock as this to increase their violence. He was dressing her arm when she began to recover; and when she opened her eyes, in a state of half-consciousness, the first object she beheld was his face bending over her. Recalling nothing of what had occurred, it seemed to her, in the dreamy condition in which the fit had left her, the same face, unchanged, which had once shone in upon her tardy springtime, and promised to ripen it into summer. She forgot it had departed and left her in the wintry cold.

And so she uttered wild words of love and trust; and the youth, while stung with remorse at his own neglect, was astonished to perceive the poetic forms of beauty in which the soul of the uneducated maiden burst into flower. But as her senses recovered themselves, the face gradually changed to her, as if the slow alteration of two years had been phantasmagorically compressed into a few moments; and the glow departed from the maiden's thoughts and words, and her soul found itself at the narrow window of the present, from which she could behold but a dreary country. From the street came the iambic cry of the fool, 'Come hame, come hame.'

Tycho Brahe, I think, is said to have kept a fool, who frequently sat at his feet in his study, and to whose mutterings he used to listen in the pauses of his own thought. The shining soul of the astronomer drew forth the rainbow of harmony from the misty spray of words ascending ever from the dark gulf into which the thoughts of the idiot were ever falling. He beheld curious concurrences of words therein, and could read strange meanings from them – sometimes even received wondrous hints from the direction of celestial inquiry, from what, to any other, and it may be to the fool himself, was but a ceaseless and aimless babble. Such power lieth in words.

It is not then to be wondered at that the sounds I have mentioned should fall on the ears of Elsie, at such a moment, as a message from God Himself. This then – all this dreariness – was but a passing show like the rest, and there lay somewhere for her a reality – a home. The tears burst up from her oppressed heart. She received the message, and prepared to go home. From that time her strength gradually sank, but her spirits as steadily rose.

The strength of the fool, too, began to fail, for he was old. He bore all the signs of age, even to the grey hairs, which betokened no wisdom. But one cannot say what wisdom might be in him, or how far he had not fought his own battle, and been victorious. Whether any notion of a continuance of life and thought dwelt in his brain, it is impossible to tell; but he seemed to have the idea that this was not his home; and those who saw him gradually approaching his end might well anticipate for him a higher life in the world to come.

He had passed through this world without ever awaking to such a consciousness of being as is common to mankind. He had spent his years like a weary dream through a long night, – a strange, dismal, unkindly dream; and now the morning was at hand. Often in his dream had he listened with sleepy senses to the ringing of the bell, but that bell would awake him at last. He was like a seed buried too deep in the soul, to which the light has never penetrated, and which, therefore, has never forced its way upwards to the open air, never experienced the resurrection of the dead. But seeds will grow ages after they have fallen into the earth; and indeed with many kinds, and within some limits, the older the seed before it germinates, the more plentiful the fruit. And may it not be believed of many human beings, that, the great Husbandman having sown them like seeds in the soil of human affairs, there they lie buried a life long; and only after the upturning of the soil by death, reach a position in which the awakening of their aspiration and the consequent growth become possible? Surely He has made nothing in vain.

A violent cold and cough brought him at last near to his end, and hearing that he was ill, Elsie ventured one bright spring day to go to see him. When she entered the miserable room where he lay, he held out his hand to her with something like a smile, and muttered feebly and painfully, 'I'm gaein' to the wow, nae to come back again.'

Elsie could not restrain her tears; while the old man, looking fixedly at her, though with meaningless eyes, muttered, for the last time, *'Come hame! come hame!'* and sank into a lethargy, from which nothing could rouse him, till, next morning, he was waked by friendly death from the long sleep of this world's night. They bore him to his favourite churchyard, and buried him within the site of the old church, below his loved bell, which had ever been to him as the cuckoo-note of a coming spring. Thus he at length obeyed its summons, and went home.

Elsie lingered till the first summer days lay warm on the land. Several kind hearts in the village, hearing of her illness, visited her and ministered to her. Wondering at her sweetness and patience they regretted they had not known her before. How much consolation might not their kindness have imparted, and how much might not their sympathy have strengthened her on her painful road!

But they could not long have delayed her going home. Nor, mentally constituted as she was, would this have been at all to be desired. Indeed it was chiefly the expectation of departure that quieted and soothed her tremulous nature. It is true that a deep spring of hope and faith kept singing on in her heart, but this alone, without the anticipation of speedy release, could only have kept her mind at peace. It could not have reached, at least for a long time, the border land between body and mind, in which her disease lay.

One still night of summer, the nurse who watched by her bedside heard her murmur through her sleep, 'I hear it: *come hame – come hame*. I'm comin', I'm comin' – I'm gaein' hame to the wow, nae to come back.'

She awoke at the sound of her own words, and begged the nurse to convey to her brother her last request, that she might be buried by the side of the fool, within the old church of Ruthven. Then she turned her face to the wall, and in the morning was found quiet and cold. She must have died within a few minutes after her last words. She was buried according to her request; and thus she too went home.

Side by side rest the aged fool and the young maiden; for the bell called them, and they obeyed; and surely they found the fire burning bright, and heard friendly voices, and felt sweet lips on theirs, in the home to which they went. Surely both intellect and love were waiting them there.

Still the old bell hangs in the old gable; and whenever another is borne to the old churchyard, it keeps calling to those who are left behind, with the same sad but friendly and unchanging voice – '*Come hame! come hame! come hame!*'

ALLAN CUNNINGHAM

THE HAUNTED SHIPS

ALONG the sea of Solway, romantic on the Scottish side, with its woodland, its bays, its cliffs, and headlands; and interesting on the English side, with its many beautiful towns with their shadows on the water, rich pastures, safe harbours, and numerous ships; there still linger many traditional stories of a maritime nature, most of them connected with superstitions singularly wild and unusual. To the curious these tales afford a rich fund of entertainment, from the many diversities of the same story; some dry and barren, and stripped of all the embellishments of poetry; others dressed out in all the riches of a superstitious belief and haunted imagination.

In this they resemble the inland traditions of the peasants; but many of the oral treasures of the Galwegian or the Cumbrian coast have the stamp of the Dane and the Norseman upon them, and claim but a remote or faint affinity with the legitimate legends of Caledonia. Something like a rude prosaic outline of several of the most noted of the northern ballads, the adventures and depredations of the old ocean kings, still lends life to the evening tale; and, among others, the story of the Haunted Ships is still popular among the maritime peasantry.

One fine harvest evening, I went on board the shallop of Richard Faulder, of Allanbay; and, committing ourselves to the waters, we allowed a gentle wind from the east to waft us at its pleasure towards the Scottish coast. We passed the sharp promontory of Siddick; and skirting the land within a stonecast, glided along the shore till we came within sight of the ruined Abbey of Sweetheart. The green mountain of Criffel ascended beside us; and the bleat of the flocks from its summit, together with the winding of the evening horn of the reapers, came softened into something like music over land and sea.

We pushed our shallop into a deep and wooded bay, and sat silently looking on the serene beauty of the place. The moon glimmered in her rising through the tall shafts of the pines of Caerlaverock; and the sky, with scarce a cloud, showered down on wood and headland and bay, the twinkling beams of a thousand stars rendering every object visible. The tide, too, was coming with that swift and silent swell observable when the wind is gentle; the woody curves along the land were filling with the flood, till it touched the green branches of the drooping trees; while in the centre current the roll and the plunge of a thousand pellocks told to the experienced fisherman that salmon were abundant.

As we looked, we saw an old man emerging from a path that winded to the shore through a grove of doddered hazel; he carried a halve-net on his back, while behind him came a girl, bearing a small harpoon with which the fishers are remarkably dexterous in striking their prey. The senior seated himself on a large grey stone, which overlooked the bay, laid aside his bonnet, and submitted his bosom and neck to the refreshing sea breeze; and taking his harpoon from his attendant, sat with the gravity and composure of a spirit of the flood, with his ministering nymph behind him. We pushed our shallop to the shore, and soon stood at their side.

'This is old Mark Macmoran the mariner, with his granddaughter Barbara,' said Richard Faulder, in a whisper that had something of fear in it; 'he knows every creek and cavern and quicksand in Solway – has seen the Spectre Hound that haunts the Isle of Man; has heard him bark, and at every bark has seen a ship sink; and he has seen, too, the Haunted Ships in full sail; and, if all tales be true, he has sailed in them himself; – he's an awful person.'

Though I perceived in the communication of my friend something of the superstition of the sailor, I could not help thinking that common rumour had made a happy choice in singling out old Mark to maintain her intercourse with the invisible world. His hair, which seemed to have refused all intercourse with the comb, hung matted upon his shoulders; a kind of mantle, or rather blanket, pinned with a wooden skewer round his neck, fell mid-leg down, concealing all his nether garments as far as a pair of hose, darned with yarn of all conceivable colours, and a pair of shoes, patched and repaired till nothing of the original structure remained, and clasped on his feet with two massy silver buckles.

If the dress of the old man was rude and sordid, that of his granddaughter was gay, and even rich. She wore a bodice of fine wool, wrought round the bosom with alternate leaf and lily, and a kirtle of the same fabric, which, almost touching her white and delicate ankle, showed her snowy feet, so fairy-light and round, that they scarcely seemed to touch the grass where she stood. Her hair, a natural ornament which woman seeks much to improve, was of bright glossy brown, and encumbered rather than adorned with a snood, set thick with marine productions, among which the small clear pearl found in the Solway was conspicuous.

Nature had not trusted to a handsome shape and a sylph-like air, for young Barbara's influence over the heart of man; but had bestowed a pair of large bright blue eyes, swimming in liquid light, so full of love and gentleness and joy, that all the sailors from Annanwater to far Saint Bees acknowledged their power, and sung songs about the bonnie lass of Mark Macmoran. She stood holding a small gaff-hook of polished steel in her hand, and seemed not dissatisfied with the glances I bestowed on her from time to time, and which I held more than requited by a single glance of those eyes which retained so many capricious hearts in subjection.

The tide, though rapidly augmenting, had not yet filled the bay at our feet. The moon now streamed fairly over the tops of Caerlaverock pines, and showed the expanse of ocean dimpling and swelling, on which sloops and shallops came dancing, and displaying at every turn their extent of white sail against the beam of the moon. I looked on old Mark the mariner, who, seated motionless on his grey stone, kept his eye fixed on the increasing waters with a look of seriousness and sorrow in which I saw little of the calculating spirit of a mere fisherman. Though he looked on the coming tide, his eyes seemed to dwell particularly on the black and decayed hulls of two vessels, which, half immersed in the quicksand, still addressed to every heart a tale of shipwreck and desolation. The tide wheeled and foamed around them; and, creeping inch by inch up the side, at last fairly threw its waters over the top, and a long and hollow eddy showed the resistance which the liquid element received.

The moment they were fairly buried in the water, the old man clasped his hands together, and said:

'Blessed be the tide that will break over and bury ye for ever! Sad to mariners, and sorrowful to maids and mothers, has the time been you have choked up this deep and bonnie bay. For evil were you sent, and for evil have you continued. Every season finds from you its song of sorrow and wail, its funeral processions, and its corpses. Woe to the land where the wood grew that made ye! Cursed be the axe that hewed ye on the mountains, the hands that joined ye together, the bay that ye first swam in, and the wind that wafted ye here! Seven times have ye put my life in peril, three fair sons have ye swept from my side, and two bonnie grand-bairns; and now, even now, your waters foam and flash for my destruction, did I venture my infirm limbs in quest of food in your deadly bay. I see by that ripple and that foam, and hear by the sound and singing of your surge, that ye yearn for another victim; but it shall not be me nor mine.'

Even as the old mariner addressed himself to the wrecked ships, a young man appeared at the southern extremity of the bay, holding his halve-net in his hand, and hastening into the current. Mark rose and shouted, and waved him back from a place which, to a person unacquainted with the dangers of the bay, real and superstitious, seemed sufficiently perilous: his granddaughter, too, added her voice to his, and waved her white hands; but the more they strove, the faster advanced the peasant, till he stood to his middle in the water, while the tide increased every moment in depth and strength.

'Andrew, Andrew,' cried the young woman, in a voice quavering with emotion, 'turn, turn, I tell you! O the Ships, the Haunted Ships!'

But the appearance of a fine run of fish had more influence with the peasant than the voice of bonnie Barbara, and forward he dashed, net in hand. In a moment he was borne off his feet, and mingled like foam with the water, and hurried towards the fatal eddies which whirled and roared round the sunken ships. But he was a powerful young man, and an expert swimmer: he seized on one of the projecting ribs of the nearest hulk, and clinging to it with the grasp of despair, uttered yell after yell, sustaining himself against the prodigious rush of the current.

From a shealing of turf and straw, within the pitch of a bar from the spot where we stood, came out an old woman bent with age, and leaning on a crutch.

'I heard the voice of that lad Andrew Lammie; can the chield be drowning, that he skirls sae uncannilie?' said the old woman, seating herself on the ground, and looking earnestly at the water. 'Oy ay,' she continued, 'he's doomed, he's doomed; heart and hand can never save him; boats, ropes, and man's strength and wit, all vain! vain! – he's doomed, he's doomed!'

By this time I had thrown myself into the shallop, followed reluctantly by Richard Faulder, over whose courage and kindness of heart supersition had great power; and with one push from the shore, and some exertion in sculling, we came within a quoit cast of the unfortunate fisherman. He stayed not to profit by our aid; for, when he perceived us near, he uttered a piercing shriek of joy, and bounded towards us through the agitated element, the full length of an oar. I saw him for a second on the surface of the water; but the eddying current sucked him down; and all I ever beheld of him again was his hand held above the flood and clutching in agony at some imaginary aid.

I sat gazing in horror on the vacant sea before us; but a breathing-time before, a human being, full of youth, and strength and hope, was there: his cries were still ringing in my ears, and echoing in the woods; and now nothing was seen or heard save the turbulent expanse of water, and the sound of its chafing on the shores. We pushed back our shallop, and resumed our station on the cliff beside the old mariner and his descendant.

'Wherefor sought ye to peril your own lives fruitlessly,' said Mark, 'in attempting to save the doomed? Whoso touches those infernal ships, never survives to tell the tale. Woe to the man who is found nigh them at midnight when the tide has subsided, and they arise in their former beauty, with forecastle, and deck, and sail, and pennon, and shroud! Then is seen the streaming of lights along the water from their cabin windows, and then is heard the sound of mirth, the clamour of tongues, and the infernal whoop and halloo, and song, ringing far and wide. Woe to the man who comes nigh them!'

To all this my Allanbay companion listened with a breathless attention. I felt something touched with a superstition to which I partly believed I had seen one victim offered up; and I inquired of the old mariner, 'How and when came these Haunted Ships there? To me they seem but the melancholy relics of some unhappy voyagers, and much more likely to warn people to shun destruction than entice and delude them to it.'

'And so,' said the old man with a smile, which had more of sorrow in it than of mirth; 'and so, young man, these black and shattered hulks seem to the eye of the multitude. But things are not what they seem: that water, a kind and convenient servant to the wants of man, which seems so smooth and so dimpling and so gentle, has swallowed up a human soul even now; and the place which it covers, so fair and so level, is a faithless quicksand, out of which none escape. Things are otherwise than they seem. Had you lived as long as I have had the sorrow to live; had you seen the storms, and braved the perils, and endured the distresses which have befallen me; had you sat gazing out on the dreary ocean at midnight on a haunted coast; had you seen comrade after comrade, brother after brother, and son after son, swept away by the merciless ocean from your very side; had you seen the shapes of friends, doomed to the wave and the quicksand, appearing to you in the dreams and visions of the night; then would your mind have been prepared for crediting the maritime legends of mariners; and the two haunted Danish ships would have had their terrors for you, as they have for all who sojourn on this coast.

'Of the time and the cause of their destruction,' continued the old man, 'I know nothing certain: they have stood as you have seen them for uncounted time; and while all other ships wrecked on this unhappy coast have gone to pieces, and rotted and sunk away in a few years, these two haunted hulks have neither sunk in the quicksand, nor has a single spar or board been displaced. Maritime legend says, that two ships of Denmark having had permission, for a time, to work deeds of darkness and dolour on the deep, were at last condemned to the whirlpool and the sunken rock, and were wrecked in this bonnie bay, as a sign to seamen to be gentle and devout. The night when they were lost was a harvest evening of uncommon mildness and beauty: the sun had newly set; the moon came brighter and brighter out; and the reapers, laying their sickles at the root of the standing corn, stood looking at the increasing magnitude of the waters, for sea and land were visible from Saint Bees to Barnhourie.

'The sails of two vessels were soon seen bent for the Scottish coast; and, with a speed outrunning the swiftest ship, they approached the dangerous quicksands and headland of Borranpoint. On the deck of the foremost ship not a living soul was seen, or shape, unless something in darkness and form resembling a human shadow could be called a shape, which flitted from extremity to extremity of the ship, with the appearance of trimming the sails, and directing the vessel's course. But the decks of its companion were crowded with human shapes; the captain and mate, and sailor and cabin-boy, all seemed there; and from them the sound of mirth and minstrelsy echoed over land and water. The coast which they skirted along was one of extreme danger, and the reapers shouted to warn them to beware of sandbank and rock; but of this friendly counsel no notice was taken, except that a large and famished dog, which sat on the prow, answered every shout with a long, loud, and melancholy howl. The deep sandbank of Carsethorn was expected to arrest the career of these desperate navigators; but they passed, with the celerity of water-fowl, over an obstruction which had wrecked many pretty ships.

'Old men shook their heads, and departed, saying, "We have seen the fiend sailing in a bottomless ship; let us go home and pray"; but one young and wilful man said, "Fiend! I'll warrant it's nae fiend, but douce Janet Withershins the witch, holding a carouse with some of her Cumberland cummers, and mickle red wine will be spilt atween them. Dod I would gladly have a toothfu'!

I'll warrant it's nane o' your cauld sour slae-water like a bottle of Bailie Skrinkie's port, but right drap-o'-my-heart's blood-stuff, that would waken a body out of their last linen. I wonder where the cummers will anchor their craft?" "And I'll vow," said another rustic, "the wine they quaff is none of your visionary drink, such as a drouthie body has dished out to his lips in a dream; nor is it shadowy and unsubstantial, like the vessels they sail in, which are made out of a cockel-shell or a cast-off slipper, or the paring of a seaman's right thumb-nail. I once got a hansel out of a witch's quaigh myself – auld Marion Mathers, of Dustiefoot, whom they tried to bury in the old kirkyard of Dunscore; but the cummer raise as fast as they laid her down, and naewhere else would she lie but in the bonnie green kirkyard of Kier, among douce and sponsible fowk. So I'll vow that the wine of a witch's cup is as fell liquor as ever did a kindly turn to a poor man's heart; and be they fiends, or be they witches, if they have red wine asteer, I'll risk a drouket sark for ae glorious tout on't." "Silence, ye sinners," said the minister's son of a neighbouring parish, who united in his own person his father's lack of devotion with his mother's love of liquor. "Whist! – speak as if ye had the fear of something holy before ye. Let the vessels run their own way to destruction: who can stay the eastern wind, and the current of the Solway sea? I can find ye Scripture warrant for that; so let them try their strength on Blawhooly rocks, and their might on the broad quicksand. There's a surf running there would knock the ribs together of a galley built by the imps of the pit, and commanded by the Prince of Darkness. Bonnilie and bravely they sail away there, but before the blast blows by they'll be wrecked; and red wine and strong brandy will be as rife as dyke water, and we'll drink the health of bonnie Bell Blackness out of her left-foot slipper."

'The speech of the young profligate was applauded by several of his companions, and away they flew to the bay of Blawhooly, from whence they never returned. The two vessels were observed all at once to stop in the bosom of the bay, on the spot where their hulls now appear; the mirth and the minstrelsy waxed louder than ever, and the forms of maidens, with instruments of music and wine-cups in their hands, thronged the decks. A boat was lowered; and the same shadowy pilot who conducted the ships made it start towards the shore with the rapidity of lightning, and its head knocked against the bank where the four young men stood who longed for the unblest drink. They leaped in with a laugh, and with a laugh were they welcomed on deck; wine-cups were given to each, and as they raised them to their lips the vessels melted away beneath their feet; and one loud shriek, mingled with laughter still louder, was heard over land and water for many miles. Nothing more was heard or seen till the morning, when the crowd who came to the beach saw with fear and wonder the two Haunted Ships, such as they now seem, masts and tackle gone; nor mark, nor sign, by which their name, country, or destination could be known, was left remaining. Such is the tradition of the mariners; and its truth has been attested by many whose sons and whose fathers have been drowned in the haunted bay of Blawhooly.'

'And trow ye,' said the old woman, who, attracted from her hut by the drowning cries of the young fisherman, had remained an auditor of the mariner's legend; 'and trow ye, Mark Macmoran, that the tale of the Haunted Ships is done? I can say no to that. Mickle have mine ears heard; but more mine eyes have witnessed since I came to dwell in this humble home by the side of the deep sea. I mind the night weel: it was on Hallowmass Eve: the nuts were cracked, and the apples were eaten, and spell and charm were tried at my fireside; till, wearied with diving into the dark waves of futurity, the lads and lasses fairly took to the more visible blessings of kind words, tender clasps, and gentle courtship. Soft words in a maiden's ear, and a kindlie kiss o' her lip, were old world matters to me, Mark Macmoran; though I mean not to say that I have been free of the folly of daunering and daffin with a youth in my day, and keeping tryste with him in dark and lonely places.

'However, as I say, these times of enjoyment were passed and gone with me – the mair's the pity that pleasure should fly sae fast away – and as I could nae make sport I thought I should not mar any; so out I sauntered into the fresh cold air, and sat down behind that old oak, and looked abroad on the wide sea. I had my ain sad thoughts, ye may think, at the time; it was in that very bay my blythe good man perished, with seven more in his company; and on that very bank where ye see the waves leaping and foaming, I saw seven stately corses streeked, but the dearest was the eighth. It was a woeful sight to me, a widow, with four bonnie boys, with nought to support them but these twa hands, and God's blessing, and a cow's grass. I have never liked to live out of sight of this bay since that time; and mony's the moonlight night I sit looking on these watery mountains, and these waste shores; it does my heart good, whatever it may do to my head. So ye see it was Hallowmass Night, and looking on sea and land sat I; and my heart wandering to other thoughts soon made me forget my youthful company at hame. It might be near the howe hour of the night. The tide was making, and its singing brought strange old world stories with it, and I thought on the dangers that sailors endure, the fates they meet with, and the fearful forms they see. My own blythe good man had seen sights that made him grave enough at times, though he aye tried to laugh them away.

'Aweel, atween that very rock aneath us and the coming tide, I saw, or thought I saw – for the tale is so dreamlike, that the whole might pass for a vision of the night – I saw the form of a man: his plaid was grey, his face was grey; and his hair, which hung low down till it nearly came to the middle of his back, was as white as the white sea-foam. He began to howk and dig under the bank; an' God be near me, thought I, this maun be the unblessed spirit of auld Adam Gowdgowpin the miser, who is doomed to dig for shipwrecked treasure, and count how many millions are hidden for ever from man's enjoyment. The form found something which in shape and hue seemed a left-foot slipper of brass; so down to the tide he marched, and placing it on the water, whirled it thrice round, and the infernal slipper dilated at every turn, till it became a bonnie barge with its sails bent, and on board leaped the form, and scudded swiftly away. He came to one of the Haunted Ships, and striking it with his oar, a fair ship, with mast and canvas and mariners, started up; he touched the other Haunted Ship, and produced the like transformation; and away the three spectre ships bounded, leaving a track of fire behind them on the billows which was long unextinguished. Now was nae that a bonnie and a fearful sight to see beneath the light of the Hallowmass moon?

'But the tale is far frae finished, for mariners say that once a year, on a certain night, if ye stand on the Borron Point, ye will see the infernal shallops coming snoring through the Solway, ye will hear the same laugh and song and mirth and minstrelsy which our ancestors heard; see them bound over the sandbanks and sunken rocks like sea-gulls, cast their anchor in Blawhooly Bay, while the shadowy figure lowers down the boat, and augments their numbers with the four unhappy mortals to whose memory a stone stands in the kirkyard, with a sinking ship and a shoreless sea cut upon it. Then the spectre ships vanish, and the drowning shriek of mortals and the rejoicing laugh of fiends are heard, and the old hulls are left as a memorial that the old spiritual kingdom has not departed from the earth. But I maun away, and trim my little cottage fire, and make it burn and blaze up bonnie, to warm the crickets and my cold and crazy bones, that maun soon be laid aneath the green sod in the eerie kirkyard.'

And away the old dame tottered to her cottage, secured the door on the inside, and soon the hearth-flame was seen to glimmer and gleam through the keyhole and window.

'I'll tell ye what,' said the old mariner, in a subdued tone, and with a shrewd and suspicious glance of his eye after the old sibyl, 'it's a word that may not very well be uttered, but there are many mistakes made in evening stories if old Moll Moray there, where she lives, knows not mickle more than she is willing to tell of the Haunted Ships, and their unhallowed mariners. She lives cannilie and quietly; no one knows how she is fed or supported; but her dress is aye whole, her cottage ever smokes, and her table lacks neither of wine, white and red, nor of fowl and fish, and white bread and brown. It was a dear scoff to Jock Matheson, when he called old Moll the uncannie carline of Blawhooly: his boat ran round and round in the centre of the Solway – everybody said it was enchanted – and down it went head foremost: and had nae Jock been a swimmer equal to a sheldrake, he would have fed the fish. But I'll warrant it sobered the lad's speech; and he never reckoned himself safe till he made auld Moll the present of a new kirtle and a stone of cheese.'

'O father,' said his granddaughter Barbara, 'ye surely wrong poor old Mary Moray: what use could it be to an old woman like her, who has no wrongs to redress, no malice to work out against mankind, and nothing to seek of enjoyment save a cannie hour and a quiet grave – what use could the fellowship of fiends and the communion of evil spirits be to her? I know Jenny Primrose puts rowan-tree above the door-head when she sees old Mary coming; I know the good wife of Kittlenaket wears rowan-berry leaves in the headband of her blue kirtle, and all for the sake of averting the unsonsie glance of Mary's right ee; and I know that the auld Laird of Burntroutwater drives his seven cows to their pasture with a wand of witch-tree, to keep Mary from milking them. But what has all that to do with haunted shallops, visionary mariners, and bottomless boats? I have heard myself as pleasant a tale about the Haunted Ships and their unworldly crews, as any one would wish to hear in a winter evening. It was told me by young Benjie Macharg, one summer night, sitting on Arbiglandbank: the lad intended a sort of love meeting: but all that he could talk of was about smearing sheep and shearing sheep, and of the wife which the Norway elves of the Haunted Ships made for his uncle Sandie Macharg. And I shall tell ye the tale as the honest lad told it to me.

'Alexander Macharg, besides being the laird of three acres of peatmoss, two kale gardens, and the owner of seven good milch cows, a pair of horses, and six pet sheep, was the husband of one of

66

the handsomest women in seven parishes. Many a lad sighed the day he was brided; and a Nithsdale laird and two Annandale moorland farmers drank themselves to their last linen, as well as their last shilling, through sorrow for her loss. But married was the dame; and home she was carried, to bear rule over her home and her husband, as an honest woman should.

'Now ye maun ken that though the flesh and blood lovers of Alexander's bonnie wife all ceased to love and to sue her after she became another's, there were certain admirers who did not consider their claim at all abated, or their hopes lessened by the kirk's famous obstacle of matrimony. Ye have heard how the devout minister of Tinwald had a fair son carried away, and bedded against his liking to an unchristened bride, whom the elves and the fairies provided: ye have heard how the bonnie bride of the drunken Laird of Soukitup was stolen by the fairies out at the back-window of the bridal chamber, the time the bridegroom was groping his way to the chamber-door; and ye have heard – but why need I multiply cases? Such things in the ancient days were as common as candlelight. So ye'll no hinder certain water elves and sea fairies, who sometimes keep festival and summer mirth in these old haunted hulks, from falling in love with the weel-faured wife of Laird Macharg; and to their plots and contrivances they went how they might accomplish to sunder man and wife; and sundering such a man and such a wife was like sundering the green leaf from the summer, or the fragrance from the flower.

'So it fell on a time that Laird Macharg took his halve-net on his back, and his steel spear in his hand, and down to Blawhooly Bay gade he, and into the water he went right between the two haunted hulks, and placing his net awaited the coming of the tide. The night, ye maun ken, was mirk, and the wind lowne, and the singing of the increasing waters among the shells and the pebbles was heard for sundry miles. All at once light began to glance and twinkle on board the two Haunted Ships from every hole and seam, and presently the sound as of a hatchet employed in squaring timber echoed far and wide. But if the toil of these unearthly workmen amazed the laird, how much more was his amazement increased when a sharp shrill voice called out, "Ho! brother, what are you doing now?" A voice still shriller responded from the other haunted ship, 'I'm making a wife to Sandie Macharg!" And a loud quavering laugh running from ship to ship, and from bank to bank, told the joy they expected from their labour.

'Now the laird, besides being a devout and a God-fearing man, was shrewd and bold; and in plot and contrivance, and skill in conducting his designs, was fairly an overmatch for any dozen land elves: but the water elves are far more subtle; besides, their haunts and their dwellings being in the great deep, pursuit and detection is hopeless if they succeed in carrying their prey to the waves. But ye shall hear. Home flew the laird, collected his family around the hearth, spoke of the signs and the sins of the times, and talked of mortification and prayer for averting calamity; and finally, taking his father's Bible, brass clasps, black print, and covered with calf-skin, from the shelf, he proceeded without let or stint to perform domestic worship. I should have told ye that he bolted and locked the door, shut up all inlet to the house, threw salt into the fire, and proceeded in every way like a man skilful in guarding against the plots of fairies and fiends. His wife looked on all this with wonder; but she saw something in her husband's looks that hindered her from intruding either question or advice, and a wise woman was she.

'Near the mid-hour of the night the rush of a horse's feet was heard, and the sound of a rider leaping from its back, and a heavy knock came to the door, accompanied by a voice, saying, "The cummer drink's hot, and the knave bairn is expected at Laird Laurie's to-night; sae mount, good-wife, and come."

' "Preserve me!" said the wife of Sandie Macharg; "that's news indeed! who could have thought it? The laird has been heirless for seventeen years! Now Sandie, my man, fetch me my skirt and hood."

'But he laid his arm round his wife's neck, and said, "If all the lairds in Galloway go heirless, over this door threshold shall you not stir to-night; and I have said, and I have sworn it: seek not to know why or wherefor – but, Lord, send us thy blessed mornlight." The wife looked for a moment in her husband's eyes, and desisted from further entreaty.

' "But let us send a civil message to the gossips, Sandy; and hadnae ye better say I am sair laid with a sudden sickness? – though it's sinful-like to send the poor messenger a mile agate with a lie in his mouth without a glass of brandy."

' "To such a messenger, and to those who sent him, no apology is needed," said the austere laird; "so let him depart." And the clatter of a horse's hoofs was heard, and the muttered imprecations of its rider on the churlish treatment he had experienced.

' "Now, Sandie, my lad," said his wife, laying an arm particularly white and round about his neck as she spoke, "are you not a queer man and a stern? I have been your wedded wife now these three years; and, beside my dower, have brought you three as bonnie bairns as ever smiled aneath a summer sun. O man, you a douce man, and fitter to be an elder than even Wille Greer himself, I have the minister's ain word for't, to put on these hard-hearted looks, and gang waving your arms that way, as if ye said, "I winna take the counsel of sic a hempie as you"; I'm your ain leal wife, and will and maun have an explanation.'

'To all this Sandie Macharg replied, "It is written – 'Wives, obey your husbands'; but we have been strayed in our devotion, so let us pray"; and down he knelt: his wife also, for she was as devout as bonnie; and beside them knelt their household, and all lights were extinguished.

' "Now this beats a'," muttered his wife to herself; "however, I shall be obedient for a time; but if I dinna ken what all this is for before the morn by sunket-time, my tongue is nae langer a tongue, nor my hands worth wearing."

'The voice of her husband in prayer interrupted this mental soliloquy; and ardently did he beseech to be preserved from the wiles of the fiends and the snares of Satan; "from witches, ghosts, goblins, elves, fairies, spunkies, and water-kelpies; from the spectre shallop of Solway; from spirits visible and invisible; from the Haunted Ships and their unearthly tenants; from maritime spirits that plotted against godly men, and fell in love with their wives – "

' "Nay, but His presence be near us!" said his wife in a low tone of dismay. "God guide my gudeman's wits: I never heard such a prayer from human lips before. But Sandie, my man, Lord's sake, rise. What fearful light is this? Barn and byre and stable maun be in a blaze; and Hawkie, and Hurley, Doddie, and Cherrie, and Damson-plum will be smoored with reek, and scorched with flame."

'And a flood of light, but not so gross as a common fire, which ascended to heaven and filled all the court before the house, amply justified the good wife's suspicions. But to the terrors of fire Sandie was as immovable as he was to the imaginary groans of the barren wife of Laird Laurie; and he held his wife, and threatened the weight of his right hand – and it was a heavy one – to all who ventured abroad, or even unbolted the door. The neighing and prancing of horses, and the bellowing of cows, augmented the horrors of the night; and to any one who only heard the din, it seemed that the whole onstead was in a blaze, and horses and cattle perishing in the flame. All wiles, common or extraordinary, were put in practice to entice or force the honest farmer and his wife to open the door; and when the like success attended every new stratagem, silence for a little while ensued and a long, loud, and shrilling laugh wound up the dramatic efforts of the night.

'In the morning, when Laird Macharg went to the door, he found standing against one of the pilasters a piece of black ship oak, rudely fashioned into something like human form, and which skilful people declared would have been clothed with seeming flesh and blood, and palmed upon him by elfin adroitness for his wife, had he admitted his visitants. A synod of wise men and women sat upon the woman of timber, and she was finally ordered to be devoured by fire, and that in the open air. A fire was soon made, and into it the elfin sculpture was tossed from the prongs of two pairs of pitchforks. The blaze that arose was awful to behold; and hissings and burstings and loud cracklings and strange noises were heard in the midst of the flame; and when the whole sank into ashes, a drinking-cup of some precious metal was found; and this cup, fashioned no doubt by elfin skill, but rendered harmless by the purification with fire, the sons and daughters of Sandie Macharg and his wife drink out of to this very day. Bless all bold men, say I, and obedient wives!'

W. E. AYTOUN

HOW WE GOT UP THE GLENMUTCHKIN RAILWAY AND HOW WE GOT OUT OF IT

I WAS confoundedly hard up. My patrimony, never of the largest, had been for the last year on the decrease – a herald would have emblazoned it, 'ARGENT, a moneybag improper, in detriment' – and though the attenuating process was not excessively rapid, it was, nevertheless, proceeding at a steady ratio. As for the ordinary means and appliances by which men contrive to recruit their exhausted exchequers, I knew none of them. Work I abhorred with a destination worthy of a scion of nobility; and, I believe, you could just as soon have persuaded the lineal representative of the Howards or Percys to exhibit himself in the character of a mountebank, as have got me to trust my person on the pinnacle of a three-legged stool. The rule of three is all very well for base mechanical souls; but I flatter myself I have an intellect too large to be limited to a ledger. 'Augustus,' said my poor mother to me, while stroking my hyacinthine tresses, one fine morning, in the very dawn and budding-time of my existence – 'Augustus, my dear boy, whatever you do, never forget that you are a gentleman.' The maternal maxim sunk deeply into my heart, and I never for a moment have forgotten it.

Notwithstanding this aristocratical resolution, the great practical question 'How am I to live!' began to thrust itself unpleasantly before me. I am one of that unfortunate class who have neither uncles nor aunts. For me, no yellow liverless individuals, with characteristic bamboo and pigtail – emblems of half-a-million – returned to his native shores from Ceylon or remote Penang. For me, no venerable spinster hoarded in the Trongate, permitting herself few luxuries during a long-protracted life, save a lass and a lanthorn, a parrot, and the invariable baudrons of antiquity. No such luck was mine. Had all Glasgow perished by some vast epidemic, I should not have found myself one farthing the richer. There would have been no golden balsam for me in the accumulated woes of Tradestown, Shettleston, and Camlachie. The time has been when – according to Washington Irving and other veracious historians – a young man had no sooner got into difficulties than a guardian angel appeared to him in a dream, with the information that at such and such a bridge, or under such and such a tree, he might find, at a slight expenditure of labour, a gallipot secured with bladder, and filled with glittering tomauns; or in the extremity of despair, the youth had only to append himself to a cord, and straightaway the other end thereof, forsaking its staple in the roof, would disclose amidst the fractured ceiling the glories of a profitable pose. These blessed days have long since gone by – at any rate, no such luck was mine. My guardian angel was either woefully ignorant of metallurgy or the stores had been surreptitiously ransacked; and as to the other expedient, I frankly confess I should have liked some better security for its result, than the precedent of the 'Heir of Lynn.'

It is a great consolation amidst all the evils of life, to know that, however bad your circumstances may be, there is always somebody else in nearly the same predicament. My chosen friend and ally, Bob M'Corkindale, was equally hard up with myself, and, if possible, more averse to exertion. Bob was essentially a speculative man – that is, in a philosophical sense. He had once got hold of a stray volume of Adam Smith, and muddled his brains for a whole week over the intricacies of the *Wealth of Nations*. The result was a crude farrago of notions regarding the true nature of money, the soundness of currency, and relative value of capital, with which he nightly favoured an admiring audience at 'The Crow'; for Bob was by no means – in the literal acceptation of the word – a dry philosopher. On the contrary, he perfectly appreciated the merits of each distinct distillery; and was understood to be the compiler of a statistical work entitled, *A Tour through the Alcoholic Districts of Scotland*. It had very early occurred to me, who knew as much of political economy as of the bagpipes, that a gentleman so well versed in the art of accumulating national wealth, must have some remote ideas of applying his principles profitably on a smaller scale. Accordingly, I gave M'Corkindale an unlimited invitation to my lodgings; and, like a good hearty fellow as he was, he availed himself every evening of the license; for I had laid in a fourteen-gallon cask of Oban whisky, and the quality of the malt was undeniable.

These were the first glorious days of general speculation. Railroads were emerging from the hands of the greater into the fingers of the lesser capitalists. Two successful harvests had given a fearful stimulus to the national energy; and it appeared perfectly certain that all the populous towns would be united, and the rich agricultural districts intersected, by the magical bands of iron. The columns of the newspapers teemed every week with the parturition of novel schemes; and the shares were no sooner announced than they were rapidly subscribed for. But what is the use of my saying anything more about the history of last year? Every one of us remembers it perfectly well. It was a capital year on the whole, and put money into many a pocket. About that time, Bob and I commenced operations. Our available capital, or negotiable bullion, in the language of my friend, amounted to about three hundred pounds, which we set aside as a joint fund for speculation. Bob, in a series of learned discourses, had convinced me that it was not only folly, but a positive sin, to leave this sum lying in the bank at a pitiful rate of interest, and otherwise unemployed, whilst every one else in the kingdom was having a pluck at the public pigeon. Somehow or other, we were unlucky in our first attempts. Speculators are like wasps; for when they have once got hold of a ripening and peach-like project, they keep it rigidly for their own swarm, and repel the approach of interlopers. Notwithstanding all our efforts, and very ingenious ones they were, we never, in a single instance, succeeded in procuring an allocation of original shares; and though we did now and then make a hit by purchase, we more frequently bought at a premium, and parted with our scrip at a discount. At the end of six months, we were not twenty pounds richer than before.

'This will never do,' said Bob, as he sat one evening in my rooms compounding his second tumbler. 'I thought we were living in an enlightened age; but I find I was mistaken. That brutal spirit of monopoly is still abroad and uncurbed. The principles of free-trade are utterly forgotten, or misunderstood. Else how comes it that David Spreul received but yesterday an allocation of two hundred shares in the Westermidden Junction; whilst your application and mine, for a thousand each, were overlooked? Is this a state of things to be tolerated? Why should he, with his fifty thousand pounds, receive a slapping premium, whilst our three hundred of available capital remains unrepresented? The fact is monstrous, and demands the immediate and serious interference of the legislature.'

'It is a bloody shame,' I said, fully alive to the manifold advantages of a premium.

'I'll tell you what, Dunshunner,' rejoined M'Corkindale. 'It's no use going on in this way. We haven't shown half pluck enough. These fellows consider us as snobs, because we don't take the bull by the horns. Now's the time for a bold stroke. The public are quite ready to subscribe for anything – and we'll start a railway for ourselves.'

'Start a railway with three hundred pounds of capital!'

'Pshaw, man! you don't know what you're talking about – we've a great deal more capital than that. Have not I told you seventy times over, that everything a man has – his coat, his hat, the tumblers he drinks from, nay, his very corporeal existence – is absolute marketable capital? What do you call that fourteen-gallon cask, I should like to know?'

'A compound of hoops and staves, containing about a quart and a half of spirits – you have effectually accounted for the rest.'

'Then it has gone to the fund of profit and loss, that's all. Never let me hear you sport those old theories again. Capital is indestructible, as I am ready to prove to you any day, in half an hour. But let us sit down seriously to business. We are rich enough to pay for the advertisements, and that is all we need care for in the mean time. The public is sure to step in, and bear us out hand-somely with the rest.'

'But where in the face of the habitable globe shall the railway be? England is out of the question, and I hardly know of a spot in the Lowlands that is not occupied already.'

'What do you say to a Spanish scheme – the Alcantara Union? Hang me if I know whether Alcantara is in Spain or Portugal; but nobody else does, and the one is quite as good as the other. Or what would you think of the Palermo Railway, with a branch to the sulphur mines? – that would be popular in the North – or the Pyrenees Direct? They would all go to a premium.'

'I must confess I should prefer a line at home.'

'Well, then, why not try the Highlands? There must be lots of traffic there in the shape of sheep, grouse, and Cockney tourists, not to mention salmon and other et-ceteras. Couldn't we tip them a railway somewhere in the west?'

'There's Glenmutchkin, for instance – '

'Capital, my dear fellow! Glorious? By Jove, first-rate!' shouted Bob in an ecstasy of delight. 'There's a distillery there, you know, and a fishing-village at the foot – at least there used to be six years ago, when I was living with the exciseman. There may be some bother about the population, though. The last laird shipped every mother's son of the aboriginal Celts to America; but, after all, that's not of much consequence. I see the whole thing! Unrivalled scenery – stupendous waterfalls – herds of black cattle – spot where Prince Charles Edward met Macgrugar of Glengrugar and his clan! We could not possibly have lighted on a more promising

74

place. Hand us over that sheet of paper, like a good fellow, and a pen. There is no time to be lost, and the sooner we get out the prospectus the better.'

'But, heaven bless you, Bob, there's a great deal to be thought of first. Who are we to get for a provisional committee?'

'That's very true,' said Bob, musingly. 'We *must* treat them to some respectable names, that is, good sounding ones. I'm afraid there is little chance of our producing a Peer to begin with?'

'None whatever – unless we could invent one, and that's hardly safe – *Burke's Peerage* has gone through too many editions. Couldn't we try the Dormants?'

'That would be rather dangerous in the teeth of the standing orders. But what do you say to a baronet? There's Sir Polloxfen Tremens. He got himself served the other day to a Nova Scotia baronetcy, with just as much title as you or I have; and he has sported the riband, and dined out on the strength of it ever since. He'll join us at once, for he has not a sixpence to lose.'

'Down with him, then,' and we headed the Provisional list with the pseudo Orange-tawny.

'Now,' said Bob, 'it's quite indispensable, as this is a Highland line, that we should put forward a Chief or two. That has always a great effect upon the English, whose feudal notions are rather of the mistiest, and principally derived from Waverley.'

'Why not write yourself down as the Laird of M'Corkindale?' said I. 'I daresay you would not be negatived by a counter-claim.'

'That would hardly do,' replied Bob, 'as I intend to be Secretary. After all, what's the use of thinking about it? Here goes for an extempore Chief'; and the villain wrote down the name of Tavish M'Tavish of Invertavish.

'I say, though,' said I, 'we must have a real Highlander on the list. If we go on this way, it will become a Justiciary matter.'

'You're devilish scrupulous, Gus,' said Bob, who, if left to himself, would have stuck in the names of the heathen gods and goddesses, or borrowed his directors from the Ossianic chronicles, rather than have delayed the prospectus. 'Where the mischief are we to find the men? I can think of no others likely to go the whole hog, can you?'

'I don't know a single Celt in Glasgow except old M'Closkie, the drunken porter at the corner of Jamaica Street.'

'He's the very man! I suppose, after the manner of his tribe, he will do anything for a pint of whisky. But what shall we call him? Jamaica Street, I fear, will hardly do for a designation.'

'Call him THE M'CLOSKIE. It will be sonorous in the ears of the Saxon!'

'Bravo!' and another Chief was added to the roll of the clans.

'Now,' said Bob, 'we must put you down. Recollect, all the management – that is, the allocation – will be intrusted to you. Augustus – you haven't a middle name, I think? – well, then, suppose we interpolate "Reginald", it has a smack of the Crusades. Augustus Reginald Dunshunner, Esq. of – where, in the name of Munchausen?'

'I'm sure I don't know. I never had any land beyond the contents of a flower-pot. Stay – I rather think I have a superiority somewhere about Paisley.'

'Just the thing,' cried Bob. 'It's heritable property, and therefor titular. What's the denomination?'

'St Mirrens.'

'Beautiful! Dunshunner of St Mirrens, I give you joy! Had you discovered that a little sooner – and I wonder you did not think of it – we might both of us have had lots of allocations. These are not the times to conceal hereditary distinctions. But now comes the serious work. We must have one or two men of known wealth upon the list. The chaff is nothing without a decoy-bird. Now, can't you help me with a name?'

'In that case,' said I, 'the game is up, and the whole scheme exploded. I would as soon undertake to evoke the ghost of Croesus.'

'Dunshunner,' said Bob very seriously, 'to be a man of information, you are possessed of marvellous few resources. I am quite ashamed of you. Now listen to me. I have thought deeply upon this subject, and am quite convinced that, with some little trouble, we may secure the co-operation of a most wealthy and influential body – one, too, that is generally supposed to have stood aloof from all speculation of the kind, and whose name would be a tower of strength in the moneyed quarters. I allude,' continued Bob, reaching across for the kettle, 'to the great Dissenting Interest.'

'The what?' cried I, aghast.

'The great Dissenting Interest. You can't have failed to observe the row they have lately been making about Sunday travelling and education. Old Sam Sawley, the coffin-maker, is their principal spokesman here; and wherever he goes the rest will follow, like a flock of sheep bounding after a patriarchal ram. I propose, therefore, to wait upon him tomorrow, and request his co-operation in a scheme which is not only to prove profitable, but to make head against the lax principles of the present age. Leave me alone to tickle him. I consider his name, and those of one or two others belonging to the same meeting-house – fellows with bank-stock, and all sorts of tin, as perfectly secure. These dissenters smell a premium from an almost incredible distance. We can fill up the rest of the committee with ciphers, and the whole thing is done.'

'But the engineer – we must announce such an officer as a matter of course.'

'I never thought of that,' said Bob. 'Couldn't we hire a fellow from one of the steamboats?'

'I fear that might get us into trouble. You know there are such things as gradients and sections to be prepared. But there's Watty Solder, the gas-fitter, who failed the other day. He's a sort of civil engineer by trade, and will jump at the proposal like a trout at the tail of a May fly.'

'Agreed. Now, then, let's fix the number of shares. This is our first experiment, and I thing we ought to be moderate. No sound political economist is avaricious. Let us say twelve thousand, at twenty pounds a-piece.'

'So be it.'

'Well, then, that's arranged. I'll see Sawley and the rest tomorrow; settle with Solder, and then write out the prospectus. You look in upon me in the evening, and we'll revise it together. Now, by your leave, let's have in the Welsh rabbit and another tumbler to drink success and prosperity to the Glenmutchkin Railway.'

I confess that, when I rose on the morrow, with a slight headache and a tongue indifferently parched, I recalled to memory, not without perturbation of conscience, and some internal qualms, the conversation of the previous evening. I felt relieved, however, after two spoonfuls of carbonate of soda, and a glance at the newspaper, wherein I perceived the announcement of no less than four other schemes equally preposterous with our own. But, after all, what right had I to assume that the Glenmutchkin project would prove an ultimate failure? I had not a scrap of statistical information that might entitle me to form such an opinion. At any rate, Parliament, by substituting the Board of Trade as an initiating body of inquiry, had created a responsible tribunal, and freed us from the chance of obloquy. I saw before me a vision of six months' steady gambling, at manifest advantage, in the shares, before a report could possibly be pronounced, or our proceedings be in any way overhauled. Of course I attended that evening punctually at my friend M'Corkindale's. Bob was in high feather; for Sawley no sooner heard of the principles upon which the railway was to be conducted, and his own nomination as a director, than he gave in his adhesion, and promised his unflinching support to the uttermost. The Prospectus ran as follows:

DIRECT GLENMUTCHKIN RAILWAY
In 12,000 Shares of £20 each. Deposit £1 per Share.
Provisional Committee
SIR POLLOXFEN TREMENS, Bart. of Toddymains.
TAVISH M'TAVISH of Invertavish.
THE M'CLOSKIE.
AUGUSTUS REGINALD DUNSHUNNER, Esq., of St Mirrens.
SAMUEL SAWLEY, Esq., Merchant.
MHIC-MHAC-VICH-INDUIBH.
PHELIM O'FINLAN, Esq., of Castle-rook, Ireland.
THE CAPTAIN of M'ALCOHOL.
FACTOR for GLENTUMBLERS.
JOHN JOB JOBSON, Esq., Manufacturer.
EVAN M'CLAW of Glenscart and Inveryewky.
JOSEPH HECKLES, Esq.
HABBAKUK GRABBIE, Portioner in Ramoth-Drumclog.
Engineer – WALTER SOLDER, Esq.
Interim-Secretary – ROBERT M'CORKINDALE, Esq.

'The necessity of a direct line of Railway communication through the fertile and populous district known as the VALLEY of GLENMUTCHKIN, has been long felt and universally acknowledged. Independently of the surpassing grandeur of its mountain scenery, which shall immediately be referred to, and other considerations of even greater importance, GLENMUTCHKIN is known to the capitalist as the most important BREEDING STATION in the Highlands of Scotland, and indeed as the great emporium from which the southern markets are supplied. It has been calculated by a most eminent authority, that every acre in the strath is capable of rearing twenty head of cattle; and, as has been ascertained after a careful admeasurement, that there are not less than TWO HUNDRED THOUSAND improvable acres immediately contiguous to the proposed line of Railway, it may confidently be assumed that the number of cattle to be conveyed along the line will amount to FOUR MILLIONS annually, which, at the lowest estimate, would yield a revenue larger, in proportion to the capital subscribed, than that of any Railway as yet completed within the United Kingdom. From this estimate the traffic in Sheep and Goats, with which the mountains are literally covered, has been carefully excluded, it having been found quite impossible (from its extent) to compute the actual revenue to be drawn from that most important branch. It may, however, be roughly assumed as from seventeen to nineteen *per cent* upon the whole, after deduction of the working expenses.

'The population of Glenmutchkin is extremely dense. Its situation on the west coast has afforded it the means of direct communication with America, of which for many years the inhabitants have actively availed themselves. Indeed, the amount of exportation of live stock from this part of the Highlands to the Western continent, has more than once attracted the attention of Parliament. The Manufacturers are large and comprehensive, and include the most famous distilleries in the world. The Minerals are most abundant, and amongst these may be reckoned quartz, porphyry, felspar, malachite, manganese, and basalt.

'At the foot of the valley, and close to the sea, lies the important village known as the CLACHAN of INVERSTARVE. It is supposed by various eminent anitquaries to have been the capital of the Picts, and, amongst the busy inroads of commercial prosperity, it still retains some interesting traces of its former grandeur. There is a large fishing station here, to which vessels from every nation resort, and the demand for foreign produce is daily and steadily increasing.

'As a sporting country Glenmutchkin is unrivalled; but is it by the tourists that its beauties will most greedily be sought. These consist of every combination which plastic nature can afford – cliffs of unusual magnitude and grandeur – waterfalls only second to the sublime cascades of Norway – woods, of which the bark is a remarkably valuable commodity. It need scarcely be added, to rouse the enthusiasm inseparable from this glorious glen, that here, in 1745, Prince Charles Edward Stuart, then in the zenith of his hopes, was joined by the brave Sir Grugar M'Grugar at the head of this devoted clan.

'The Railway will be twelve miles long, and can be completed within six months after the Act of Parliament is obtained. The gradients are easy, and the curves obtuse. There are no viaducts of any importance, and only four tunnels along the whole length of the line. The shortest of these does not exceed a mile and a half.

'In conclusion, the projectors of this Railway beg to state that they have determined, as a principle, to set their face AGAINST ALL SUNDAY TRAVELLING WHATSOEVER, and to oppose EVERY BILL which may hereafter be brought into Parliament, unless it shall contain a clause to that effect. It is also their intention to take up the cause of the poor and neglected STOKER, for whose accommodation, and social, moral, religious, and intellectual improvement, a large stock of evangelical tracts will speedily be required. Tenders of these, in quantities of not less than 12,000 may be sent in to the Interim Secretary. Shares must be applied for within ten days from the present date.

By order of the Provisional Committee,
ROBT. M'CORKINDALE, *Secretary.*

'There!' said Bob, slapping down the prospectus on the table, with the jauntiness of a Cockney vouchsafing a Pint of Hermitage to his guests – 'What do you think of that? If it doesn't do the business effectually, I shall submit to be called a Dutchman. That last touch about the stoker will bring us in the subscriptions of the old ladies by the score.'

'Very masterly, indeed ' said I. 'But who the deuce is Mhic-Mhac-vich-Induibh?'

'A *bona fide* chief, I assure you, though a little reduced: I picked him up upon the Broomielaw. His grandfather had an island somewhere to the west of the Hebrides; but it is not laid down in the maps.'

'And the Captain of M'Alcohol?'

'A crack distiller.'

'And the Factor for Glentumblers?'

'His principal customer. But, bless you, my dear St Mirrens! don't bother yourself any more about the committee. They are as respectable a set – on paper at least – as you would wish to see of a summer's morning, and the beauty of it is that they will give us no manner of trouble. Now about the allocation. You and I must restrict ourselves to a couple of thousand shares a-piece. That's only a third of the whole, but it won't do to be greedy.'

'But, Bob, consider! Where on earth are we to find the money to pay up the deposits?'

'Can you, the principal director of the Glenmutchkin Railway, ask me, the secreatry, such a question? Don't you know that any of the banks will give us tick to the amount of "half the deposits." All that is settled already, and you can get your two thousand pounds whenever you please merely for the signing of a bill. Sawley must get a thousand according to stipulation – Jobson, Heckles, and Grabbie, at least five hundred a-piece, and another five hundred, I should think, will exhaust the remaining means of the committee. So that, out of our whole stock, there remain just five thousand shares to be allocated to the speculative and evangelical public. My eyes! won't there be a scramble for them!'

Next day our prospectus appeared in the newspapers. It was read, canvassed, and generally approved of. During the afternoon, I took an opportunity of looking into the Tontine, and whilst under shelter of the *Glasgow Herald*, my ears were solaced with such ejaculations as the following:

'I say, Jimsy, hae ye seen this grand new prospectus for a railway tae Glenmutchkin?'

'Ay – it looks no that ill. The Hieland lairds are pitting their best fit foremost. Will ye apply for shares?'

'I think I'll tak' twa hundred. Wha's Sir Polloxfen Tremens?'

'He'll be yin o' the Ayrshire folk. He used to rin horses at the Paisley races.'

('The devil he did!' thought I.)

'D'ye ken ony o' the directors, Jimsy?'

'I ken Sawley fine. Ye may depend on't, it's a gude thing if he's in't, for he's a howkin' body.'

'Then it's sure to gae up. What prem. d'ye think it will bring?'

'Twa pund a share, and maybe mair.'

' 'Od, I'll apply for three hundred!'

'Heaven bless you, my dear countrymen!' thought I as I sallied forth to refresh myself with a basin of soup, 'do but maintain this liberal and patriotic feeling – this thirst for national improvement, internal communication, and premiums – a short while longer, and I know whose fortune will be made.'

On the following morning my breakfast-table was covered with shoals of letters, from fellows whom I scarcely ever had spoken to – or who, to use a franker phraseology, had scarcely ever condescended to speak to me – entreating my influence as a director to obtain them shares in the new undertaking. I never bore malice in my life, so I chalked them down, without favouritism, for a certain proportion. Whilst engaged in this charitable work, the door flew open, and M'Corkindale, looking utterly haggard with excitement, rushed in.

'You may buy an estate whenever you please, Dunshunner,' cried he, 'the world's gone perfectly mad! I have been to Blazes the broker, and he tells me that the whole amount of the stock has been subscribed for four times over already, and he has not yet got in the returns from Edinburgh and Liverpool!'

'Are they good names though, Bob – sure cards – none of your M'Closkies, and M'Alcohols?'

'The first names in the city, I assure you, and most of them holders for investment. I wouldn't take ten millions for their capital.'

'Then the sooner we close the list the better.'

'I think so too. I suspect a rival company will be out before long. Blazes says the shares are selling already conditionally on allotment, at seven-and-sixpence premium.'

'The deuce they are! I say, Bob, since we have the cards in our hands, would it not be wise to favour them with a few hundred at that rate? A bird in the hand, you know, is worth two in the bush, eh?'

'I know no such maxim in political economy,' replied the secretary. 'Are you mad, Dunshunner? How are the shares ever to go up, if it gets wind that the directors are selling already? Our business just now, is to *bull* the line, not to *bear* it; and if you will trust me, I shall show them such an operation on the ascending scale, as the Stock Exchange has not witnessed for this long and many a day. Then, to-morrow, I shall advertise in the papers that the committee, having received applications for ten times the amount of stock, have been compelled, unwillingly, to close the lists. That will be a slap in the face to the dilatory gentlemen, and send up the shares like wildfire.'

Bob was right. No sooner did the advertisement appear, than a simultaneous groan was uttered by some hundreds of disappointed speculators, who with unwonted and unnecessary caution had been anxious to see their way a little before committing themselves to our splendid enterprise. In consequence, they rushed into the market, with intense anxiety to make what terms they could at the earliest stage, and the seven-and-sixpence of premium was doubled in the course of a forenoon.

The allocation passed over very peaceably. Sawley, Heckles, Jobson, Grabbie, and the Captain of M'Alcohol, besides myself, attended, and took part in the business. We were also threatened with the presence of the M'Closkie and Vich-Induibh; but M'Corkindale, entertaining some reasonable doubts as the effect which their corporeal appearance might have upon the representatives of the dissenting interest, had taken the precaution to get them snugly housed in a tavern, where an unbounded supply of gratuitous Ferintosh deprived us of the benefit of their experience. We, however, allotted them twenty shares a-piece. Sir Polloxfen Tremens sent a handsome, though rather illegible letter of apology, dated from an island in Lochlomond, where he was said to be detained on particular business.

Mr Sawley, who officiated as our chairman, was kind enough,

before parting, to pass a very flattering eulogium upon the excellence and candour of all the preliminary arrangements. It would now, he said, go forth to the public that this line was not, like some others he could mention, a mere bubble, emanating from the stank of private interest, but a solid, lasting superstructure, based upon the principles of sound return for capital, and serious evangelical truth (hear, hear). The time was fast approaching, when the gravestone, with the words 'HIC OBIIT' chiselled upon it, would be placed at the head of all the other lines which rejected the grand opportunity of conveying education to the stoker. The stoker, in his (Mr Sawley's) opinion, had a right to ask the all-important question, 'Am I not a man and a brother?' (Cheers). Much had been said and written lately about a work, called *Tracts for the Times*. With the opinions contained in that publication he was not conversant, as it was conducted by persons of another community from that to which he (Mr Sawley) had the privilege to belong. But he hoped very soon, under the auspices of the Glenmutchkin Railway Company, to see a new periodical established, under the title of *Tracts for the Trains*. He never for a moment would relax his efforts to knock a nail into the coffin, which, he might say, was already made, and measured, and cloth-covered for the reception of all establishments; and with these sentiments, and the conviction that the shares must rise, could it be doubted that he would remain a fast friend to the interests of this Company for ever? (much cheering).

After having delivered this address, Mr Sawley affectionately squeezed the hands of his brother directors, leaving several of us much overcome. As, however, M'Corkindale had told me that every one of Sawley's shares had been disposed of in the market the day before, I felt less compunction at having refused to allow that excellent man an extra thousand beyond the amount he had applied for, not withstanding of his broadest hints, and even private entreaties.

'Confound the greedy hypocrite!' said Bob; 'does he think we shall let him Burke the line for nothing? No – no! let him go to the brokers and buy his shares back, if he thinks they are likely to rise. I'll be bound he has made a cool five hundred out of them already.'

On the day which succeeded the allocation, the following entry appeared in the Glasgow share-lists. 'Direct Glenmutchkin Railway 15s. 15s. 6d. 15s. 6d. 16s. 15s. 6d. 16s. 16s. 6d. 16s. 6d. 16s. 17s. 18s. 18s. 19s. 6d. 21s. 21s. 22s. 6d. 24s. 25s. 6d. 27s. 29s. 29s. 6d. 30s. 31s. pm.'

'They might go higher, and they ought to go higher,' said Bob musingly; 'but there's not much more stock to come and go upon, and these two share-sharks, Jobson and Grabbie, I know, will be in the market tomorrow. We must not let them have the whip-hand of us. I think upon the whole, Dunshunner, though it's letting them go dog cheap, that we ought to sell half our shares at the present premium, whilst there is a certainty of getting it.'

'Why not sell the whole? I'm sure I have no objections to part with every stiver of the scrip on such terms.'

'Perhaps,' said Bob, 'upon general principles you might be right; but then remember that we have a vested interest in the line.'

'Vested interest be hanged!'

'That's very well – at the same time it is no use to kill your salmon in a hurry. The bulls have done their work pretty well for us, and we ought to keep something on hand for the bears; they are snuffing at it already. I could almost swear that some of those fellows who have sold today are working for a time-bargain.'

We accordingly got rid of a couple of thousand shares, the proceeds of which not only enabled us to discharge the deposit loan, but left us a material surplus. Under these circumstances, a two-hand banquet was proposed and unanimously carried, the commencement of which I distinctly remember, but am rather dubious as to the end. So many stories have lately been circulated to the prejudice of railway directors, that I think it my duty to state that this entertainment was scrupulously defrayed by ourselves, and *not* carried to account, either of the preliminary survey, or the expense of the provisional committee.

Nothing effects so great a metamorphosis in the bearing of the outer man as a sudden change of fortune. The anemone of the garden differs scarcely more from its unpretending prototype of the woods, than Robert M'Corkindale, Esq., Secretary and Projector of the Glenmutchkin Railway, differed from Bob M'Corkindale, the seedy frequenter of 'The Crow'. In the days of yore, men eyed the surtout – napless at the velvet collar, and preternaturally white at the seams – which Bob vouchsafed to wear, with looks of dim suspicion, as if some faint reminiscence, similar to that which is said to recall the memory of a former state of existence, suggested to them a notion that the garment had once been their own. Indeed, his whole appearance was then wonderfully second-hand. Now he had cast his slough. A most undeniable Taglioni, with trimmings just bordering upon frogs, gave dignity to his demeanour and twofold amplitude to his chest. The horn eyeglass was exchanged for one of purest gold, the dingy high-lows for well-waxed Wellingtons, the Paisley fogle for the fabric of the China loom. Moreover, he walked with a swagger, and affected in common conversation a peculiar dialect which he opined to be the purest English, but which no one – except a bagman – could be reasonably expected to understand. His pockets were invariably crammed with share-lists; and he quoted, if he did not comprehend, the money article from *The Times*. This sort of assumption, though very ludicrous in itself, goes down wonderfully. Bob gradually became a sort of authority, and his opinions got quoted on 'Change. He was no ass, notwithstanding his peculiarities, and made good use of his opportunity.

For myself, I bore my new dignities with an air of modest meekness. A certain degree of starchness is indispensable for a railway director, if he means to go forward in his high calling and prosper; he must abandon all juvenile eccentricities, and aim at the appearance of a decided enemy to free trade in the article of Wild Oats. Accordingly, as the first step towards respectability, I eschewed coloured waistcoats, and gave out that I was a marrying man. No man under forty, unless he is a positive idiot, will stand forth as a theoretical bachelor. It is all nonsense to say that there is anything unpleasant in being courted. Attention, whether from male or female, tickles the vanity; and although I have a reasonable, and I hope, not unwholesome regard for the gratification of my other appetites, I confess that this same vanity is by far the most poignant of the whole. I therefore surrendered myself freely to the soft allurements thrown in my way by such matronly denizens of Glasgow as were possessed of stock in the shape of marriageable daughters; and walked the more readily into their toils, because every party, though nominally for the purposes of tea, wound up with a hot supper, and something hotter still by way of assisting the digestion.

I don't know whether it was my determined conduct at the allocation, my territorial title, or a most exaggerated idea of my circumstances, that worked upon the mind of Mr Sawley. Possibly it was a combination of the three; but sure enough few days had elapsed before I received a formal card of invitation to a tea and serious conversation. Now serious conversation is a sort of thing that I never shone in, possibly because my early studies were framed in a different direction; but as I really was unwilling to offend the respectable coffin-maker, and as I found that the Captain of M'Alcohol – a decided trump in his way – had also received a summons, I notified my acceptance.

M'Alochol and I went together. The Captain, an enormous browny Celt, with superhuman whiskers, and a shock of the fieriest hair, had figged himself out, *more majorum*, in the full Highland costume. I never saw Rob Roy on the stage look half so dignified or ferocious. He glittered from head to foot, with dirk, pistol, and skean-dhu, and at least a hundredweight of cairngorms cast a prismatic glory around his person. I felt quite abashed beside him.

We were ushered into Mr Sawley's drawing-room. Round the walls, and at considerable distances from each other, were seated about a dozen characters, male and female, all of them dressed in sable, and wearing countenances of woe. Sawley advanced, and wrung me by the hand with so piteous an expression of visage, that I could not help thinking some awful catastrophe had just befallen his family.

'You are welcome, Mr Dunshunner – welcome to my humble tabernacle. Let me present you to Mrs Sawley' – and a lady, who seemed to have bathed in the Yellow Sea, rose from her seat, and favoured me with a profound curtsy.

'My daughter – Miss Selina Sawley.'

I felt in my brain the scorching glance of the two darkest eyes it ever was my fortune to behold, as the beauteous Selina looked up from the perusal of her handkerchief hem. It was a pity that the other features were not corresponding; for the nose was flat, and the mouth of such dimensions, that Harlequin might have jumped down it with impunity – but the eyes *were* splendid.

In obedience to a sign from the hostess, I sank into a chair beside Selina; and not knowing exactly what to say, hazarded some observation about the weather.

'Yes, it is indeed a suggestive season. How deeply, Mr Dunshunner, we ought to feel the pensive progress of autumn towards a soft and premature decay! I always think, about this time of the year, that nature is falling into a consumption!'

'To be sure, ma'am,' said I, rather taken aback by this style of colloquy, 'the trees are looking devilishly hectic.'

'Ah, you have remarked that too! Strange! it was but yesterday that I was wandering through Kelvin Grove, and as the phantom breeze brought down the withered foliage from the spray, I thought how probable it was that they might ere long rustle over young and glowing hearts deposited prematurely in the tomb!'

This, which struck me as a very passable imitation of Dickens's pathetic writings, was a poser. In default of language, I looked Miss Sawley straight in the face, and attempted a substitute for a sigh. I was rewarded with a tender glance.

'Ah!' said she, 'I see you are a congenial spirit. How delightful, and yet how rare it is to meet with any one who thinks in unison with yourself! Do you ever walk in the Necropolis, Mr Dunshunner? It is my favourite haunt of a morning. There we can wean ourselves, as it were, from life, and, beneath the melancholy yew and cypress, anticipate the setting star. How often there have I seen the procession – the funeral of some very, *very* little child' –

'Selina, my love,' said Mrs Sawley, 'have the kindness to ring for the cookies.'

I, as in duty bound, started up to save the fair enthusiast the trouble, and was not sorry to observe my seat immediately occupied by a very cadaverous gentleman, who was evidently jealous of the progress I was rapidly making. Sawley, with an air of great mystery, informed me that this was a Mr Dalgleish of Raxmathrapple, the representative of an ancient Scottish family who claimed an important heritable office. The name, I thought, was familiar to me, but there was something in the appearance of Mr Dalgleish which, notwithstanding the smiles of Miss Selina, rendered a rivalship in that quarter utterly out of the question.

I hate injustice, so let me do due honour in description to the Sawley banquet. The tea-urn most literally corresponded to its name. The table was decked out with divers platters, containing seed-cakes cut into rhomboids, almond biscuits, and ratafia drops. Also, on the sideboard, there were two salvers, each of which contained a congregation of glasses, filled with port and sherry. The former fluid, as I afterwards ascertained, was of the kind advertised as 'curious,' and proffered for sale at the reasonable rate of sixteen shillings per dozen. The banquet, on the whole, was rather peculiar than enticing; and, for the life of me, I could not divest myself of the idea that the selfsame viands had figured, not long before, as funeral refreshments at a dirige. No such suspicion seemed to cross the mind of M'Alcohol, who hitherto had remained uneasily surveying his nails in a corner, but at the first symptom of food started forwards, and was in the act of making a clean sweep of the china, when Sawley proposed the singular preliminary of a hymn.

The hymn was accordingly sung. I am thankful to say it was such a one as I never heard before, or expect to hear again; and unless it was composed by the Reverend Saunders Peden in an hour of paroxysm on the moors, I cannot conjecture the author. After this original symphony, tea was discussed, and after tea, to my amazement, more hot brandy-and-water that I ever remember to have seen circulated at the most convivial party. Of course this effected a radical change in the spirits and conversation of the circle. It was again my lot to be placed by the side of the fascinating Selina, whose sentimentality gradually thawed away beneath the influence of sundry sips, which she accepted with a delicate reluctance. This time Dalgleish of Raxmathrapple had not the remotest chance. M'Alcohol got furious, sang Gaelic songs, and even delivered a sermon in genuine Erse, without incurring a rebuke; whilst, for my own part, I must needs confess that I waxed unnecessarily amorous, and the last thing I recollect was the pressure of Mr Sawley's hand at the door, as he denominated me his dear boy, and hoped I would soon come back and visit Mrs Sawley and Selina. The recollection of these passages next morning was the surest antidote to my return.

Three weeks had elapsed, and still the Glenmutchkin Railway shares were at a premium, though rather lower than when we sold. Our engineer, Watty Solder, returned from his first survey of the line, along with an assistant who really appeared to have some remote glimmerings of the science and practice of mensuration. It seemed, from a verbal report, that the line was actually practicable; and the survey would have been completed in a very short time – 'If,' according to the account of Solder, 'there had been ae hoos in the glen. But ever sin' the distillery stoppit – and that was twa year last Martinmas – there wasna a hole whaur a Christian could lay his head, muckle less get white sugar to his toddy, forbye the change-house at the clachan; and the auld luckie that keepit it was sair forfochten wi' the palsy, and maist in the dead-thraws. There was naebody else living within twal miles o' the line, barring a tacksman, a lamiter, and a bauldie.'

We had some difficulty in preventing Mr Solder from making this report open and patent to the public, which premature disclosure might have interfered materially with the preparation of our traffic tables, not to mention the marketable value of the shares. We therefore kept him steadily at work out of Glasgow, upon a very liberal allowance, to which, apparently, he did not object.

'Dunshunner,' said M'Corkindale to me one day, 'I suspect that there is something going on about our railway more than we are aware of. Have you observed that the shares are preternaturally high just now?'

'So much the better. Let's sell.'

'I did this morning – both yours and mine, at two pounds ten shillings premium.'

'The deuce you did! Then we're out of the whole concern.'

'Not quite. If my suspicions are correct, there's a good deal more money yet to be got from the speculation. Somebody has been bulling the stock without orders; and, as they can have no information which we are not perfectly up to, depend upon it, it is done for a purpose. I suspect Sawley and his friends. They have never been quite happy since the allocation; and I caught him yesterday pumping our broker in the back shop. We'll see in a day or two. If they are beginning a bearing operation, I know how to catch them.'

And, in effect, the bearing operation commenced. Next day, heavy sales were affected for delivery in three weeks; and the stock, as if waterlogged, began to sink. The same thing continued for the following two days, until the premium became nearly nominal. In the mean time, Bob and I, in conjunction with two leading capitalists whom we let into the secret, bought up steadily every share that was offered; and at the end of a fortnight we found that we had purchased rather more than double the amount of the whole original stock. Sawley and his disciples, who, as M'Corkindale suspected, were at the bottom of the whole transaction, having beared to their heart's content, now came into the market to purchase, in order to redeem their engagements. The following extracts from the weekly share-lists will show the results of their endeavours to regain their lost position:

GLENMUTCHKIN RAIL., £1 paid

Sat.	Mon.	Tues.	Wed.	Thurs.	Frid.	Sat.
$1\frac{1}{8}$	$2\frac{1}{4}$	$4\frac{3}{8}$	$7\frac{1}{2}$	$10\frac{3}{4}$	$15\frac{3}{8}$	17

and Monday was the day of delivery.

I have no means of knowing in what frame of mind Mr Sawley spent the Sunday, or whether he had recourse for mental consolation to Peden; but on Monday morning he presented himself at my door in full funeral costume, with about a quarter of a mile of crape swathed round his hat, black gloves, and a countenance infinitely more doleful than if he had been attending the interment of his beloved wife.

'Walk in, Mr Sawley,' said I cheerfully. 'What a long time it is since I have had the pleasure of seeing you – too long indeed for brother directors. How are Mrs Sawley and Miss Selina – won't you take a cup of coffee?'

'Grass, sir, grass!' said Mr Sawley, with a sigh like the groan of a furnace-bellows. 'We are all flowers of the oven – weak, erring creatures, every one of us. Ah! Mr Dunshunner! you have been a great stranger at Lykewake Terrace!'

'Take a muffin, Mr Sawley. Anything new in the railway world?'

'Ah, my dear sir – my good Mr Augustus Reginald – I wanted to have some serious conversation with you on that very point. I am afraid there is something far wrong indeed in the present state of our stock.'

'Why, to be sure it is high; but that, you know, is a token of the public confidence in the line. After all, the rise is nothing compared to that of several English railways; and individually, I suppose, neither of us have any reason to complain.'

'I don't like it,' said Sawley, watching me over the margin of his coffee-cup. 'I don't like it. It savours too much of gambling for a man of my habits. Selina, who is a sensible girl, has serious qualms on the subject.'

'Then why not get out of it? I have no objection to run the risk, and if you like to transact with me, I will pay you ready money for every share you have at the present market price.'

Sawley writhed uneasily in his chair.

'Will you sell me five hundred, Mr Sawley? Say the word and it is a bargain.'

'A time bargain?' quavered the coffin-maker.

'No. Money down, and scrip handed over.'

'I – I can't. The fact is, my dear friend, I have sold all my stock already!'

'Then permit me to ask, Mr Sawley, what possible objection you can have to the present aspect of affairs? You do not surely suppose that we are going to issue new shares and bring down the market, simply because you have realised at a handsome premium?'

'A handsome premium! O Lord!' moaned Sawley.

'Why, what did you get for them?'

'Four, three, and two and a half.'

'A very considerable profit indeed,' said I; 'and you ought to be abundantly thankful. We shall talk this matter over at another time, Mr Sawley, but just now I must beg you to excuse me. I have a particular engagement this morning with my broker – rather a heavy transaction to settle – and so – '

'It's no use beating about the bush, any longer,' said Mr Sawley in an excited tone, at the same time dashing down his crape-covered castor on the floor. 'Did you ever see a ruined man with a large family? Look at me, Mr Dunshunner – I'm one, and you've done it!'

'Mr Sawley! are you in your senses?'

'That depends on circumstances. Haven't you been buying stock lately?'

'I am glad to say I have – two thousand Glenmutchkins, I think, and this is the day of delivery.'

'Well, then – can't you see how the matter stands? It was I who sold them!'

'Well!'

'Mother of Moses, sir! don't you see I'm ruined?'

'By no means – but you must not swear. I pay over the money for your scrip, and you pocket a premium. It seems to me a very simple transaction.'

'But I tell you I haven't got the scrip!' cried Sawley, gnashing his teeth, whilst the cold beads of perspiration gathered largely on his brow.

'This is very unfortunate! Have you lost it?'

'No! – the devil tempted me, and I oversold!'

There was a very long pause, during which I assumed an aspect of serious and dignified rebuke.

'Is it possible?' said I in a low tone, after the manner of Kean's offended fathers. 'What! you, Mr Sawley – the stoker's friend – the enemy of gambling – the father of Selina – condescend to so equivocal a transaction? You amaze me! But I never was the man to press heavily on a friend' – here Sawley brightened up – 'your secret is safe with me, and it shall be your own fault if it reaches the ears of the Session. Pay me over the difference at the present market price, and I release you of your obligation.'

'Then I'm in the Gazette, that's all,' said Sawley doggedly, 'and a wife and nine beautiful babes upon the parish! I had hoped other things from you, Mr Dunshunner – I thought you and Selina – '

'Nonsense, man! Nobody goes into the Gazette just now – it will be time enough when the general crash comes. Out with your cheque-book, and write me an order for four-and-twenty thousand. Confound fractions! in these days one can afford to be liberal.'

'I haven't got it,' said Sawley. 'You have no idea how bad our trade has been of late, for nobody seems to think of dying. I have not sold a gross of coffins this fortnight. But I'll tell you what – I'll give you five thousand down in cash, and ten thousand in shares – further I can't go.'

'Now, Mr Sawley,' said I, 'I may be blamed by wordly-minded persons for what I am going to do; but I am a man of principle, and feel deeply for the situation of your amiable wife and family. I bear no malice, though it is quite clear that you intended to make me the sufferer. Pay me fifteen thousand over the counter, and we cry quits for ever.'

'Won't you take Camlachie Cemetery shares? They are sure to go up.'

'No!'

'Twelve Hundred Cowcaddens' Water, with an issue of new stock next week?'

'Not if they disseminated the Ganges!'

'A thousand Ramshorn Gas – four per cent guaranteed until the act?'

'Not if they promised twenty, and melted down the sun in their retort!'

'Blawweary Iron? Best spec. going.'

'No, I tell you once for all! If you don't like my offer – and it is an uncommonly liberal one – say so, and I'll expose you this afternoon upon 'Change.'

'Well, then – there's a cheque. But may the – '

'Stop, sir! Any such profane expressions, and I shall insist upon the original bargain. So, then – now we're quits. I wish you a very good-morning, Mr Sawley, and better luck next time. Pray remember me to your amiable family.'

The door had hardly closed upon the discomfited coffin-maker, and I was still in the preliminary steps of an extempore *pas seul*, intended as the outward demonstration of exceedingly inward joy, when Bob M'Corkindale entered. I told him the result of the morning's conference.

'You have let him off too easily,' said the Political Economist. 'Had I been his creditor, I certainly should have sacked the shares into the bargain. There is nothing like rigid dealing between man and man.'

'I am contented with moderate profits,' said I; 'besides, the image of Selina overcame me. How goes it with Jobson and Grabbie?'

'Jobson has paid, and Grabbie compounded. Heckles – may he die an evil death! – has repudiated, become a lame duck, and waddled; but no doubt his estate will pay a dividend.'

'So, then, we are clear of the whole Glenmutchkin business, and at a handsome profit.'

'A fair interest for the outlay of capital – nothing more. But I'm not quite done with the concern yet.'

'How so? not another bearing operation?'

'No; that cock would hardly fight. But you forget that I am secretary of the company, and have a small account against them for services already rendered. I must do what I can to carry the bill through Parliament; and, as you have now sold your whole shares, I advise you to resign from the direction, go down straight to Glenmutchkin, and qualify yourself for a witness. We shall give you five guineas a-day, and pay all your expenses.'

'Not a bad notion. But what has become of M'Closkie, and the other fellow with the jaw-breaking name?'

'Vich-Induibh? I have looked after their interests, and in duty bound, sold their shares at a large premium, and despatched them to their native hills on annuities.'

'And Sir Polloxfen?'

'Died yesterday of spontaneous combustion.'

As the company seemed breaking up, I thought I could not do better than take M'Corkindale's hint, and accordingly betook myself to Glenmutchkin, along with the Captain of M'Alcohol, and we quartered ourselves upon the Factor for Glentumblers. We found Watty Solder very shaky, and his assistant also lapsing into habits of painful inebriety. We saw little of them except of an evening, for we shot and fished the whole day, and made ourselves remarkably comfortable. By singular good-luck, the plans and sections were lodged in time, and the Board of Trade very handsomely reported in our favour, with a recommendation of what they were pleased to call 'the Glenmutchkin system,' and a hope that it might generally be carried out. What this system was, I never clearly understood; but, of course, none of us had any objections. This circumstance gave an additional impetus to the shares, and they once more went up. I was, however too cautious to plunge a second time into Charybdis, but M'Corkindale did, and again emerged with plunder.

When the time came for the parliamentary contest, we all emigrated to London. I still recollect, with lively satisfaction, the many pleasant days we spent in the metropolis at the company's expense. There were just a neat fifty of us, and we occupied the whole of an hotel. The discussion before the committee was long and formidable. We were opposed by four other companies who patronised lines, of which the nearest was at least a hundred miles distant from Glenmutchkin; but as they founded their opposition upon dissent from 'the Glenmutchkin system' generally, the committee allowed them to be heard. We fought for three weeks a most desperate battle, and might in the end have been victorious, had not our last antagonist, at the very close of his case, pointed out no less than seventy-three fatal errors in the parliamentary plan deposited by the unfortunate Solder. Why this was not done earlier, I never exactly understood; it may be, that our opponents, with gentlemanly consideration, were unwilling to curtail our sojourn in London – and their own. The drama was now finally closed, and after all preliminary expenses were paid, sixpence per share was returned to the holders upon surrender of their scrip.

Such is an accurate history of the Origin, Rise, Progress and Fall of the Direct Glenmutchkin Railway. It contains a deep moral, if anybody has sense enough to see it; if not, I have a new project in my eye for next session, of which timely notice shall be given.

A LEGEND OF '45

'I WAS in the nursery at the time, as you can understand; but the chief person of the tale was my father's closest friend, and he was my counsellor in some kittle passes of my life in after days. He never mentioned this business himself; but my father, who knew the particulars brawly, used to tell it to me often, and he bequeathed the story to me as one of his most valuable legacies.'

The old man's face brightened, and his voice became firmer as he proceeded.

'You see yon picture hanging on the left of your mother, Balquherrie? – that was your grandfather, Hugh Outram. You see what a black-a-vice chiel he was, and I can tell you there was a fire in his een whiles that made some folk say he had the gift of second sight. At any rate, he had the pith of a giant in his arms, and the courage of a lion in his heart. He could love – like a mother; he could hate – like a jealous wife. My story is about him.

'He courted Mistress Graham, of Eskbank; he followed her night and day; he was devoted to her body and soul – in fact he was clean crack about her. But she was won by Corbet of Dowiemuir. When that became known, Hugh Outram shut himself up here in Balquherrie and would have no speech with any living creature for awhile.

'At last my father got speaking with him, and showed him the duties he was neglecting because of a disappointment that could not be helped, but could be easily enough mended. Hugh stepped out of his shell, and took up the work that was appointed for him in seeing after the welfare of those dependent on him. When he was told that Mistress Corbet had been brought to bed of a daughter, he said, "Lord, smile on the bairn," although he never could be brought to say that he forgave Corbet.

'Prince Charlie raised his standard in Glenfinnan, and Corbet was the first to place himself under it, with all whom he could influence. Hugh took arms for the Government within a few days after; but my father, who served with him, was satisfied that he decided on this course more because of his hate for the man who had won his lady than because of his regard for the house of Hanover. No doubt he had his thought of meeting him in battle, and once, at the mention of the possibility of it, my father was frightened by the fire that flamed in Hugh's een.

'Be that as it may, he did his duty well and bravely. He would have prevented Cope marching like a stray goose into the north while the rebels were, unchecked, marching on the south, but his word was not heeded at the time. The prince made a brilliant run over the country; and at length the Duke of Cumberland chased him back to Culloden, where the Stuart cause was drowned in blood.

'After the battle there were days and weeks of persistent pursuit of the fugitive rebels. The mercenary troops were pitiless; and men of our own country consented to or took part in cruelties that will shame the victory so long as the memory of them lasts. But Hugh Outram was disappointed if he had been calculating on coming across Corbet. So far they had not met.

'He had command of a company of Hessians – the most malignant, because the most indifferent, of all the pursuers – and he was in chase of a score of rebels who were making their way to the west. My father had twenty-three lads left of forty whom he had led from Pitnafour, and he was on the same track as his friend. Reports had been received that the scattered fugitives were rendezvousing in Lochaber, with the intention of making a stand yet in defence of the Stuart, in spite of what had happened. The duke was mightily wroth at this, and was not likely to show mercy to those who fell into his hands, still less to those who failed in the discharge of the savage duty entrusted to them.

'As it happened, the companies of Outram and of my father met in Glendhu, within three miles of Dowiemuir. They encamped for the night, and the two friends slept together in a shepherd's shieling. In the cold grey of morning they were aroused by a Hessian, who acquainted them that he had traced a rebel officer to a farmhouse, distant only half a mile. They marched instantly on the place, surrounded the house, and the search commenced, hot and furious.

'Nobody appeared to offer them opposition, and the house was as quiet as if there were not a living creature in it. The officers remained outside, and soon the fellow who had raised the halloo stepped out of the house, carrying a greeting bairn in his arms. After him walked a lady with hair and dress disarranged, and a face white as a fine Holland sheet, but steady as a rock.

'She pleaded with them piteously to spare the life of her bairn, and the soldiers threatened to stick it on the point of their bayonets unless she confessed where the father lay hidden.

'She begged them to spare the child, but would not answer the question. The bayonets were fixed, the bairn raised high in the arms of a big rascal as if holding it ready to be impaled.

'Still the woman pleaded, and would not hear the condition on which alone her prayer would be granted.

'They said they would count six, and then proceed to the execution if she did not yield. They began to count, and she did not flinch until she observed Outram, who was grimly watching what passed. Then she trembled to her heels and groaned, sinking on the ground, for she concluded that there was neither pity nor mercy to expect from him for the wife and infant of Corbet of Dowiemuir.

'It was the lady herself Outram was looking at: his enemy and all that was precious to him were at his mercy. No man ever had a fairer opportunity of wreaking a terrible vengeance on his foe, without moving a finger; he had only to remain silent, and he was assured of the utmost retaliation for whatever he might have suffered.

'He turned to my father, who was curious as to what he would do:

' "You must command here," he said, with big sobs in his throat, and turning his back on the scene, "but save the bairn and spare the woman."

'The child was placed on the ground beside its mother, who looked with wide parched eyes at her preserver, recognising his kindness and yet doubting him. She seemed to have lost the power of moving or speaking; but when she saw the soldiers set fire to the house at the four corners, she started, clutching the bairn to her bosom, trembling and moaning, her bloosdhot eyes leaping from her head in fright.

'When she saw the flames spring up to the thatch, and heard the burning joists crackle, she louped to her feet and walked straight over to Hugh Outram.

' "Sir," she said, "you were once my friend; it was Heaven's will that I should lose your friendship; but you are a man, and I a woman nigh mad with pain. My husband he lies in there, sick and wounded sore, so that he cannot move, and, without help, must die in the flame. You are his foe, at home and in the field; but sir, he is my husband and the father of my bairn, and – *I love him*."

'Hugh Outram stood glowering at the blaze that was working

out his worst spite. The devil bade him stand still; but he looked at the woman's face; he listened to the greeting bairn, and he made answer:

' "Madam, your husband was my worst foe, but that shall not make me the less your friend. He has taken from me my best hope, but he shall not take from me your respect or my own.'

'She first stared at him not knowing what he meant to do, and aye the house was burning, and the flames grew bigger.

'He cried to my father: "Turn your face another way, Pitna, that you may not see me. Call off the lads, haste down the glen with them, and I will deliver the traitor to you without fail."

'My father guessed what he was meaning, and in pity for the lady did not say a word to the contrary. He called the soldiers together, and making them believe that the rebel had escaped down the glen, led them away in full chase.

'Outram asked the lady where her man was hidden; she feared to answer, for she had heard him promise to deliver the traitor. He pointed to the burning house, saying: "Trust me."

'She told him what he required to know, and he marched into the house, the flames hissing at him and scorching his clothes, the beams crackling above him and tumbling about him, the smoke fluffing in his face choking and blinding him. But in spite of flame and smoke, he made his way to the hiding-place of the rebel, and found him lying as though he were already dead. Outram lifted his enemy in his arms, and carried him out from the fiery grave to the place where Mistress Corbet was on her knees, praying God to help and shield her true friend.

'He laid down him on the ground beside her. First she looked at her guidman, and saw that life was in him yet, and next she looked up at her friend, but she could not speak a word. She saw that the hair was nearly burnt off his head, and his left hand was scarred, so that it bore the mark until the day he died. She tore her gown, and tied a strip of it round his hand. Then she got water from the well and bathed her man's head and face, while the bairn was croodling on his breast.

'Outram got a horse and conveyed them five miles up the glen to a shepherd's bigging near Loch Fey – he was obliged to hold Corbet in the saddle the whole road; and there was no speech passed between them. But when he had seen them bestowed in the cot and was going away, the lady lifted up her bairn – a lassie, I ought to have told you – and bade her kiss him. The wee thing put her arms round his neck and cuddled him, and he trembled like a willow wand in a storm. Mistress Corbet stooped down with big tears in her een now and kissed his hand.

' "God will bless you, sir," was all that she could say.

'He went and looked at Corbet where he lay, helpless and insensible, but beginning to breathe in a natural way.

' "He will live," said Outram, stepping to the door, "and I hope you will be happy. Think on me whiles: I am paying a high price for a kind place in your memory – and I am content."

'She did not understand then how high the price was that he was prepared to pay; but afterwards she heard it all from my father.

'To him Outram went as fast as he could, and found him at the place where they had camped during the night.

' "I promised to deliver the traitor to you, Pitna," he said, as quietly as though there was nothing out of the ordinary in what he was doing, "and I keep faith with you. I am he – there is my sword."

'He laid the sword down, and my father took it up, after staring at him a minute, fancying he was mad.

' "I understand you," Pitna answered. "I know what you have done, and – although it was rash and perilous – damm it, sir, I think you acted nobly. Take back your sword; I can keep a secret."

' "No," said Outram, shaking his head, "that would involve you in the penalty for my treason."

'He went straight to Cumberland himself, and the duke received him graciously enough, for his repute was high.

' "What is the penalty, excellency, for an officer under your command who aids a rebel to escape?" he asked.

' "Death," cried the duke, aloud and fierce.

' "Then I yield to my fate," he said, and told what he had done.

'His Grace was furious, and Outram was arrested. But his past services pleaded for him, and the President Forbes, with other gentlemen of weight, and whose adherence to the Government was beyond doubt, joined in an appeal for clemency. The duke had not the grace to appreciate Outram's conduct, but he had discretion enough not to proceed to extremity in such a case as this. So the only punishment inflicted on Outram was the cancelling of his commission, and that he did not regard as any loss. He was liberated, and spent his days usefully at home.'

S. R. CROCKETT

THE LAMMAS PREACHING

'AND I further intimate,' said the minister, 'that I will preach this evening at Cauldshaws, and my text will be from the ninth chapter of the book of Ecclesiastes and the tenth verse, "Whatsoever thy hand findeth to do, do it with thy might." '

'Save us,' said Janet MacTaggart, 'he's clean forgotten "if it be the Lord's wull." Maybe he'll be for gaun whether it's His wull or no" – he's a sair masterfu' man, the minister; but he comes frae the Machars,* an' kens little aboot the jealous God we hae amang the hills o' Gallawa'!'

The minister continued, in the same high, level tone in which he did his preaching: 'There are a number of sluggards who lay the weight of their own laziness on the Almighty, saying, "I am a worm and no man – how should I strive with my Maker?" whenever they are at strife with their own sluggishness. There will be a word for all such this evening at the farmtown of Cauldshaws, presently occupied by Gilbert M'Kissock – public worship to begin at seven o'clock.'

The congregation of Barnessock kirk tumbled amicably over its own heels with eagerness to get into the kirkyaird in order to settle the momentous question, 'Whose back was he on the day?'

Robert Kirk, Carsethorn, had a packet of peppermint lozenges in the crown of his 'lum' hat – deponed to by Elizabeth Douglas or Barr, in Barnbogrie, whose husband, Weelum Barr, put on the hat of the aforesaid Robert Kirk by mistake for his own, whereupon the peppermints fell to the floor and rolled under the pews in most unseemly fashion. Elizabeth Kirk is of opinion that this should be brought to the notice of Session, she herself always taking her peppermint while genteelly wiping her mouth with the corner of her handkerchief. Robert Kirk, on being put to the question, admits the facts, but says that it was his wife put them there to be near her hand.

* The Eastern Lowlands of Wigtownshire

The minister, however, ever ready with his word, brought him to shame by saying, 'O Robert, Robert, that was just what Adam said, "The woman Thou gavest me, she gave me to eat!"' The aforesaid Robert Kirk thinks that it is meddling with the original Hebrew to apply this to peppermints, and also says that Elizabeth Kirk is an impident besom, and furthermore that, as all the country well knows – (Here the chronicler omits much matter actionable in the civil courts of the realm.)

'Janet,' said the minister to his housekeeper, 'I am to preach tonight at Cauldshaws on the text, "Whatsoever thy hand findeth to do, do it with thy might."'

'I ken,' said Janet, 'I saw it on yer desk. I pat it ablow the clock for fear the wun's o' heeven micht blaw it awa' like chaff, an' you couldna do wantin' it!'

'Janet MacTaggart,' said the minister tartly, 'bring in the denner, and do not meddle with what does not concern you.'

Janet could not abide read sermons; her natural woman rose against them. She knew, as she had said, that God was a jealous God, and, with regard to the minister, she looked upon herself as His vicegerent.

'He's young an' terrable ram-stam an' opeenionated – fu' o' buiklear, but wi' little gracious experience. For a' that, the root o' the maitter's in 'im,' said Janet, not unhopefully.

'I'm gaun to preach at Cauldshaws, and my text's "Whatsoever thy hand findeth to do, do it with they might,"' said the minister to the precentor that afternoon, on the manse doorstep.

'The Lord's no' in a' his thochts. I'll gang wi' the lad mysel,' said the precentor.

Now, Galloway is so much out of the world that the Almighty has not there lifted His hand from reward and punishment, from guiding and restraining, as He has done in big towns where everything goes by machinery. Man may say that there is no God when he only sees a handbreadth of smoky heaven between the chimney-pots; but out on the fields of oats and bear, and up on the screes of the hillsides, where the mother granite sticks her bleaching ribs through the heather, men have reached great assurance on this and other matters.

The burns were running red with the mighty July rain when Douglas Maclellan started over the meadows and moors to preach his sermon at the farmtown of Cauldshaws. He had thanked the Lord that morning in his opening prayer for 'the bounteous rain wherewith He had seen meet to refresh His weary heritage.'

His congregation slightly acquiesced, 'for what,' said they, 'could a man from the Machars be expected to ken about meadow hay?'

When the minister and the precentor got to the foot of the manse loaning, they came upon the parish ne'er-do-well, Ebie Kirgan, who kept himself in employment by constantly scratching his head, trying to think of something to do, and whose clothes were constructed on the latest sanitary principles of ventilation. The ruins of Ebie's hat were usually tipped over one eye for enlarged facilities of scratching in the rear.

'If it's yer wull, minister, I'll come to hear ye the nicht. It's drawing to mair rain, I'm thinkin'!' said the Scarecrow.

'I hope the discourse may be profitable to you, Ebenezer, for, as I intimated this morning, I am to preach from the text, "Whatsoever thy hand findeth to do, do it with thy might." '

'Ay, minister,' said Ebie, relieving his right hand, and tipping his hat over the other eye to give his left free play. So the three struck over the fields, making for the thorn tree at the corner, where Robert Kirk's dyke dipped into the standing water of the meadow.

'Do you think ye can manage it, Maister Maclellan?' said the precentor. 'Ye're wet halfway up the leg already.'

'An' there's sax feet o' black moss water in the Laneburn as sure as I'm a leevin' sowl,' added Ebie Kirgan.

'I'm to preach at Cauldshaws, and my text is, "Whatsoever thy hand findeth to do, do it with thy might"!' said the minister, stubbornly glooming from under the eaves of his eyebrows as the swarthy men from the Machars are wont to do. His companions said no more. They came to Camelon Lane, where usually Robert Kirk had a leaping pole on either bank to assist the traveller across, but both poles had gone down the water in the morning to look for Robert's meadow hay.

'Tak' care, Maister Maclellan, ye'll be in deep water afore ye ken. O man, ye had far better turn!'

The precentor stood up to his knees in water on what had once been the bank, and wrung his hands. But the minister pushed steadily ahead into the turbid and sluggish water.

'I canna come, oh, I canna come, for I'm a man that has a family.'

'It's no' your work; stay where ye are,' cried the minister, without looking over his shoulder; 'but as for me, I'm intimated to preach this night at Cauldshaws, and my text – '

Here he stepped into a deep hole, and his text was suddenly shut within him by the gurgle of moss water in his throat. His arms rose above the surface like the black spars of a windmill. But Ebie Kirgan sculled himself swiftly out, swimming with his shoeless feet, and pushed the minister before him to the farther bank – the water gushing out of rents in his clothes as easily as out of the gills of a fish.

The minister stood with unshaken confidence on the bank. He ran peat water like a spout in a thunder plump, and black rivulets of dye were trickling from under his hat down his brow and dripping from the end of his nose.

'Then you'll not come any farther?' he called across to the precentor.

'I canna, oh, I canna; though I'm most awful' wullin'. Kirsty wad never forgie me gin I was to droon.'

'Then I'll e'en have to raise the tune myself – though three times "Kilmarnock" is a pity,' said the minister, turning on his heel and striding away through the shallow sea, splashing the water as high as his head with a kind of headstrong glee which seemed to the precentor a direct defiance of Providence. Ebie Kirgan followed half a dozen steps behind. The support of the precentor's lay semi-equality taken from him, he began to regret that he had come, and silently and ruefully plunged along after the minister through the water-logged meadows. They came in time to the foot of Robert Kirk's march dyke, and skirted it a hundred yards upward to avoid the deep pool in which the Laneburn waters were swirling. The minister climbed silently up the seven-foot dyke, pausing a second on the top to balance himself for his leap to the other side. As he did so Ebie Kirgan saw that the dyke was swaying to the fall, having been weakened by the rush of water on the farther side. He rushed instantly at the minister, and gave him a push with both hands which caused Mr Maclellan to alight on his feet clear of the falling stones. The dyke did not so much fall outward as settle down on its own ruins. Ebie fell on his face among the stones with the impetus of his own eagerness. He arose, however, quickly – only limping slightly from what he called a 'bit chack' (nip) on the leg between the stones.

'That was a merciful Providence, Ebenezer,' said the minister, solemnly; 'I hope you are duly thankful!'

'Dod, I am that!' replied Ebie, scratching his head vigorously with his right hand and rubbing his leg with his left. 'Gin I hadna gi'en ye that dunch, ye micht hae preachen nane at Cauldshaws this nicht.'

They now crossed a fairly level clover field, dank and laid with wet. The scent of the clover rose to their nostrils with almost overpowering force. There was not a breath of air. The sky was blue and the sun shining. Only a sullen roar came over the hill, sounding in the silence like the rush of a train over a far-away viaduct.

'What is that?' queried the minister, stopping to listen.

Ebie took a brisk sidelong look at him. 'I'm some dootsome that'll be the Skyreburn coming doon off o' Cairnsmuir!'

The minister tramped unconcernedly on. Ebie Kirgan stared at him.

'He canna ken what a "Skyreburn warnin' " is – he'll be thinkin' it's some bit Machars' burn that the laddies set their whurlie mills in. But he'll turn richt eneuch when he sees Skyreburn roarin' reed in a Lammas flood, I'm thinkin'!'

They took their way over the shoulder of the hill in the beautiful evening, leaning eagerly forward to get the first glimpse of the cause of that deep and resonant roar. In a moment they saw below them a narrow rock-walled gulley, ten or fifteen yards across, filled to the brim with rushing water. It was not black peat water like the Camelon Lane, but it ran red as keel, flecked now and then with a revolving white blur as one of the Cauldshaws sheep spun downward to the sea, with four black feet turned pitifully up to the blue sky.

Ebie looked at the minister. 'He'll turn noo if he's mortal,' he said. But the minister held on. He looked at the water up and down the roaring stream. On a hill above, the farmer of Cauldshaws, having driven all his remaining sheep together, sat down to watch. Seeing the minister, he stood up and excitedly waved him back. But Douglas Maclellah from the Machars never gave him a look, and his shouting was of less effect than if he had been crying to an untrained collie.

The minister looked long up the stream, and at a point where the rocks came very close together, and many stunted pines were growing, he saw one which, having stood on the immediate brink, had been so much undercut that it leaned over the gulley like a fishing-rod. With a keen glance along its length, the minister, jamming his dripping soft felt hat on the back of his head, was setting foot on the perilous slope of the uneven red-brown trunk, when Ebie Kirgan caught him sharply by the arm.

'It's no' for me to speak to a minister at ordinar' times,' he stammered, gathering courage in his desperation; 'but, oh, man, it's fair murder to try to gang ower that water!'

The minister wrenched himself free, and sprang along the trunk with wonderful agility. 'I'm intimated to preach at Cauldshaws this night, and my text is, "Whatsoever thy hand findeth to do, do

104

it with thy might"!' he shouted.

He made his way up and up the slope of the fir tree, which, having little grip of the rock, dipped and swayed under his tread. Ebie Kirgan fell on his knees and prayed aloud. He had not prayed since his stepmother boxed his ears for getting into bed without saying his prayers twenty years ago. This had set him against it. But he prayed now, and to infinitely more purpose than his minister had recently done. But when the climber had reached the branchy top, and was striving to get a few feet farther, in order to clear the surging linn before he made his spring, Ebie rose to his feet, leaving his prayer unfinished. He sent forth an almost animal shriek of terror. The tree roots cracked like breaking cables and slowly gave way, an avalanche of stones plumped into the whirl, and the top of the fir crashed downwards on the rocks of the opposite bank.

'Oh, man, call on the name of the Lord!' cried Ebie Kirgan, the ragged preacher, at the top of his voice.

Then he saw something detach itself from the tree as it re-bounded, and for a moment rise and fall black against the sunset. Then Ebie the Outcast fell on his face like a dead man.

In the white coverleted 'room' of the farmtown of Cauldshaws a white-faced lad lay, with his eyes closed and a wet cloth on his brow. A large-boned, red-cheeked, motherly woman stole to and fro with a foot as light as a fairy. The sleeper stirred and tried to lift an unavailing hand to his head. The mistress of Cauldshaws stole to his bedside as he opened his eyes. She laid a restraining hand on him as he strove to rise.

'Let me up,' said the minister, 'I must away, for I'm intimated to preach at Cauldshaws, and my text is, "Whatsoever thy hand findeth to do, do it with thy might." '

'My bonny man,' said the goodwife tenderly, 'you'll preach best on the broad o' yer back this mony a day, an' when ye rise your best text will be, "He sent from above, He took me, and drew me out of many waters"!'

A DREAM OF DEATH

Not very long ago, one William Laidlaw, a sturdy Borderer, went on an excursion to a remote district in the Highlands of Scotland. He was a tall and very athletic man, remarkably active, and matchless at cudgel-playing, running, wrestling, and other exercises, for which the Borderers have been noted from time immemorial. To his other accomplishments he added an excellent temper, was full of good-humour, and a most capital bottle-companion.

Most of our modern travellers would have performed the greater part of the journey he undertook in a steam-boat, a stage-coach, or some such convenience; but he preferred going on foot, without any companion excepting an old oaken cudgel, which had been handed down to him from several generations, and which, by way of fancy, had been christened 'Knock-him-down.'

With his trusty friend in his hand, and fifty pounds sterling in his pocket, he found himself, by the fourth day, in one of the most dismal glens of the Highlands. It was by this time nightfall, and both William's appetite and limbs told him it was high time to look about for a place of repose, having, since six in the morning, walked nearly fifty English miles.

Now, the question which employed his cogitations at this moment, was whether he should proceed, at the risk of losing his way among the bogs and morasses for which this district is famed, or remain till daybreak where he was? Both expedients were unpleasant, and it is difficult to say which he would have adopted, when, about a mile to the left, a glimmering among the darkness attracted his notice.

It might have been a 'Will-o'-wisp,' or the light of some evil spirit at its midnight orgies; but whatever the cause might be, it decided Mr Laidlaw as to his further operations. He did not reflect a moment upon the matter, but exercising 'Knock-him-down' in its usual capacity of walking assistant, he found himself in a few minutes alongside the spot from which the light proceeded. It was a Highland cottage, built after the usual fashion, partly of stone and partly of turf; but without examining too minutely the exterior of the building, he applied the stick to the door with such a degree of force as he conceived necessary to arouse the inmates.

'Wha's there?' cried a shrill voice, like that of an old woman; 'what want ye at this hour of the night?'

'I want lodging, honest woman, if such a thing is to be got.'

'Na, na,' replied the inmate, 'you can get nae lodging here. Neither gentle nor simple shall enter my house this night. Gang on your ways, you're no aboon five miles frae the clachan of Ballacher.'

'Five deevils!' exclaimed the Borderer; 'I tell you I have walked fifty miles already, and could as soon find out Johnny Groat's as the clachan.'

'Walk fifty more, then,' cried the obstinate portress; 'but here you downa enter, while I can keep you out.'

'If you come to that, my woman,' said William, 'we shall soon settle the point. In plain language, if you do not let me in wi' your gude-will I shall enter without it,' and with that he laid his shoulder to the door, with the full intention of storming the fortress. A whispering within made him pause a moment.

'And must I let him in?' murmured the old woman to some one who seemed in the interior.

'Yes,' answered a half-suppressed voice; 'he may enter – he is but one, and we are three – a lowland tup, I suppose.'

The door was slowly opened. The person who performed this unwilling act was a woman apparently above seventy, haggard and bent by an accumulation of infirmity and years. Her face was pale, malignant, and wrinkled, and her little sharp peering eyes seemed, like those of the adder, to shoot forth evil upon whomsoever she gazed. As William entered, he encountered this aged sibyl, her natural hideousness exposed full to his gaze by the little rush-light she held up above her head, the better to view the tall Borderer.

'You want a night's lodging, say you? Ay, nae doubt, like many others frae the south, come to trouble honest folks.'

'There's nae need to talk about troubling,' said Laidlaw. 'If you have trouble you shall be paid for it; and since you are pleased, my auld lady, to talk about the south, let me say a word of the north. I have got money in my pouch to pay my way wherever I go, and this is mair than some of your bonnie Highland lairds can say. Her it lies, my lady!' and he struck with the palm of his hand the large and well-replenished pocket-book which bulged out from his side.

'I want nane of your money,' said the old crone, her eyes never-theless sparkling with a malicious joy; 'walk in; you will have the company of strangers for the night.'

He followed her advice, and went to the end of the cottage, near which, upon the floor, blazed a large fire of peat. There was no grate, and for a chimney a hole in the roof sufficed, through which the smoke ascended in large volumes. Here he saw the company mentioned by the sibyl. It consisted of three men, of the most fierce and savage aspect. Two of them were dressed as sailors, the third in a sort of Highland garb.

He had never seen any person who had so completely the air of desperadoes. The two first were dark in their complexions, their black bushy beards apparently unshorn for many weeks. Their expressions were dark and ominous, and bespoke spirits within which had been trained up in crime. Nor were the red locks of the third, and his fiery countenance, and sharp, cruel eyes, less appalling, and less indicative of evil.

So near an intercourse with such people, and under those circumstances, would have thrown a chill over most hearts; but William Laidlaw was naturally a stranger to fear, and, at any rate, his great strength gave him a confidence which it was very difficult to shake; he had, besides, a most unbounded confidence in scientific cudgel-playing, and in the virtues of 'Knock-him-down.'

These three men were seated around the fire; and when our traveller came alongside of them, and saluted them, not one returned his salutation. Each sat in dogged silence. If they deigned to recognise him, it was by looks of ferocious sternness, and these looks were momentary, for they instantly relapsed into their former state of sullen apathy.

William was at this time beset by two most unfortunate inclinations. He had an incorrigible desire, first, to speak, and secondly, to eat; and never had any propensities come upon a man so *malapropos*. He sat for a few minutes absolutely nonplussed about the method of gratifying them. At length, after revolving the matter deeply in his mind, he contrived to get out with the following words:

'I have been thinking, gudewife, that something to eat is very agreeable when a body is hungry.' No answer.

'I have been thinking, mistress, that when a man is hungry he is the better of something to eat.' No answer.

'Did you hear what I was saying, mistress?'

'Perfectly weel.'

'And what is your opinion of the matter?'

'My opinion is, that a hungry man is the better of being fed.' Such was the old dame's reply; and he thought he could perceive

108

a smile of bitter ridicule curl up the savage lips of his three neigh-bours.

'Was there ever such an auld hag?' thought the yeoman to himself. 'There she sits at her wheel, and cares nae mair for a fellow-creature than I would for a dead sheep.'

'Mistress,' continued he, 'I see you will not tak' hints. I maun then tell you plainly that I am the next door to starvation, and that I will thank you for something to eat.'

This produced the desired effect, for she instantly got up from her wheel, went to a cupboard, and produced a plentiful supply of cold venison, bread and cheese, together with a large bottle full of the finest whisky.

William now felt quite at his ease. Putting 'Knock-him-down' beside him, and planting himself at the table, he commenced operations in a style that would have done honour to Friar Tuck himself. Venison, bread and cheese disappeared like magic. So in-tently did he keep to his occupation that he neither thought nor cared about any other object.

Everything which came under the denomination of eatable having disappeared from the table, he proceeded to discuss the contents of the black bottle which stood by. He probably indulged rather freely in this respect, for shortly after commencing he be-came very talkative, and seemed resolved, at all risks, to extract conversation from his mute companions.

'You will be in the smuggling trade, frien'?' said he, slapping the shoulder of one of his dark-complexioned neighbours. The fellow started from his seat, and looked upon the Borderer with an expression of anger and menace, but he was suddenly quieted by one of his companions, who whispered into his ear, 'Hush, Roderick; never mind him; the time is not yet come.'

'I was saying, frien',' reiterated Laidlaw, without perceiving this interruption, 'that you will be in the smuggling trade?'

'Maybe I am,' was the fellow's answer.

'And you are a fish of the same water?' continued William to the second, who nodded assent.

'And you, frien', wi' the red hair, what are ye?'

'Humph!'

'Humph!' cried the Borderer; 'that is one way of answering questions – humph, ay humph, very good; ha, ha, your health, Mr Humph!' and he straightaway swallowed another glass of the potent spirit.

These three personages, during the whole of his various harangues, preserved the same unchanged silence, replying to his broken and unconnected questions by nods and monosyllables. They even held no verbal communication with one another, but each continued apparently within himself the thread of his own gloomy meditations. The night by this time waxed late; the spirit began to riot a little in the Borderer's head; and concluding that there was no sociality among persons who would neither drink nor speak, he quaffed off a final glass, and dropped back on his chair.

How long he remained in this state cannot be known. Certain it is, he was rather suddenly awakened from it by a hand working its way cautiously and gently into his bosom. At first he did not know what to make of this: his ideas were as yet unrallied, and by a sort of instinct he merely pressed his left hand against the spot by way of resistance. The same force continuing, however, to operate as formerly, he opened his eyes, and saw himself surrounded by the three strangers. The red-haired ruffian was the person who had aroused him – the two others, one of them armed with a cutlass, stood by. William was so astonished at this scene that he could form no opinion on the subject. His brain still rang with the strange visions that had crossed it, and with the influence of intoxication.

'I am thinking, honest man, that you are stealing my pocket-book,' was the first ejaculation he got out with, gazing at the same time with a bewildered look on the plunderer.

'Down with the villain!' thundered one of these worthies at the same instant; 'and you, sir,' brandishing his cutlass over the Borderer's head, 'resist, and I will cleave you to the collar.'

This exclamation acted like magic upon Laidlaw; it seemed to sober him in an instant, and point out his perilous situation.

The trio had rushed upon him, and attempted to hold him down. Now or never was the period to put his immense strength to the trial. Collecting all his energies, he bounded from their grasp, and his herculean fist falling like a sledge-hammer upon the forehead of him who carried the cutlass, the ruffian tumbled headlong to the earth. In a moment more he stood in the centre of the cottage, whirling 'Knock-him-down' around his head in the attitude of defiance. Such was now his appearance of determined courage and strength that the two ruffians opposed to him, although powerful men, and armed with bludgeons, did not dare to advance, but re-coiled several paces from their single opponent. He had escaped thus far, but his situation was still very hazardous, for the men, though baffled, kept their eyes intently fixed upon him, and seemed only to wait an opportunity when they could rush on with most advantage. Besides, the one he had floored had just got up, and with his cutlass joined the others. If they had made an attack upon him, his great skill and vigour would in all probability have brought one of them to the ground, but then he would have been assailed by the two others; and the issue of such a contest, armed as one of them was, could not but be highly dangerous.

Meanwhile the men, although none of them ventured to rush singly upon the Borderer, began to advance in a body, as if for the purpose of getting behind him.

'Now,' thought William, 'if I can but keep you quiet till I get opposite the door, I may show you a trick that will astonish you.'

So planning his scheme, he continued retreating before his assailants, and holding up his cudgel in the true scientific position till he came within a foot of the door; most fortunately it stood wide open. One step aside, and the threshold was gained – another, and it was passed.

In the twinkling of an eye, swift like a thunderbolt, fell 'Knock-him-down' upon the head of the most forward opponent, and in another out bolted William Laidlaw from the cottage. The whole was the work of an instant. He who received the blow fell stunned and bleeding to the ground, and his companions were so confounded that they stood mute and gazing at each other for several seconds. Their resolution was soon taken, and in a mood between shame and revenge, they sallied out after the fugitive. Their speed was, however, employed in vain against the fleetest runner of the Cheviots, and they were afraid to separate, lest each might encounter singly this formidable adversary, who perhaps might have dealt with them in the same manner as Horatius did with the Curiatii of old. The pursuit continued but a short way, as the yeoman more than double distanced his pursuers in the first two minutes, and left them no chance of coming up with him.

It was by this time three in the morning. The intense darkness of midnight had worn away, and though the sun was yet beneath the horizon, a sort of reflected light so far prevailed as to render near objects visible. In the course of an hour the hill tops became exposed above the misty wreaths which hung heavily upon their sides, and which began to dissolve away and float slowly down the glen in pale columns.

In a short time a hue like that of twilight rendered distinctly visible the mountain boundaries of the vale. William walked onward with his usual speed. Such at last was his prodigious rapidity of movement that he utterly lost the use of his senses. He appeared to himself to fly rather than walk over the earth; his head became giddy, and it is difficult to say where his flight might have ended,

111

when 'Knock-him-down' was suddenly swept from his hand. This in a moment arrested his speed, for such was his sympathy with his companion that he could not possibly get on, or even live without it.

'Knock-him-down, whare are ye?' was his first exclamation at the departure of his favourite. 'I say, Knock-him-down – whare are ye?' Here honest William sat down upon the heath to bemoan his misfortune. Now for the first time in his life he parted with all recollection. A strange, mysterious, indescribable ringing took place in his ears – the hills reeled – his head nodded once, twice, and again – and in a few seconds he dropped into a profound sleep.

This may be considered an epoch in the yeoman's life, for here he, for the first time, according to his own account, was visited by a dream. Out of the pale mist of the glen he imagined he saw approach him the very person to whose house he was bound. The aspect of this man was melancholy – his face deadly pale – and as he stood opposite to the Borderer and said, 'William Laidlaw,' the latter felt his flesh creep with an unutterable dread.

'William Laidlaw,' continued he, 'you are going to my house, but you will not find me at home. I have gone to a far country – Neil M'Kinnon and his two cousins sent me there. You will find my body in the pit near the Cairn of Dalgulish. The money you are bringing to me give to my poor family, and may God bless you!' Having pronounced these words the figure vanished, nor had the Borderer the power to recall it. He did not, however, awake, but lay in the same restless state till the sun, shining in all the splendour of an August morning, burst upon him.

William awoke a sober man. The morning was indeed beautiful. The sun shone in his strength, lighting up the vale with a flood of radiance. On the summits of the hills not a cloud rested – all was clear and lucid as crystal, and the untainted sky hung like a vault of pure sapphire over the thousand rocks and glens beneath.

The object which first arrested our friend's attention was 'knock-him-down' stuck up in the middle of a whin bush, and his immediate impulse was to relieve it from this inglorious situation. Having done this, stretched his limbs, and examined his pocket-book, which he found 'tight and well,' he proceeded on his journey. He was naturally the reverse of superstitious, but somehow or other a train of unpleasant thoughts came over him, which he could not get rid of. His mind was so unaccustomed to thinking of any kind, and, above all, to gloomy thinking, that he knew not what to make of the matter. He whistled and sang in vain to dispel the feeling. The same load hung upon his mind, and oppressed it grievously.

In this train he found himself at length in front of the clachan of Ballacher. This small village was in possession of the individual to whom he was journeying. His dwelling, a large farmhouse, was in the centre; the cottages which surrounded it were occupied by his servants and tenantry.

It was about mid-day when he entered the village. It was deserted, while a strange and subduing melancholy seemed to hang over it. He strode slowly on, but no human being made his appearance. At length a funeral procession, followed by many women and children, came silently up the middle avenue of the village. It might be a deception of his fancy, but he thought the looks of the mourners were more sad and more profoundly interesting than he had ever witnessed on any previous occasion. He followed the convoy to the cemetery, which was not far distant, and when the last shovelful of earth was thrown upon the grave, he inquired whose funeral it was.

'It is that of Allaster Wilson, our master,' was the reply.

'Good Heaven! and how did he die?' cried William, deeply agitated.

'That no one knows,' answered an old man who stood by; 'he was found murdered; but a day will come when the Lord will cause his blood to be requited on his murderers.'

'And where was his body found?' said the astonished Borderer.

'In the chalk-pit near the Cairn of Dalgulish,' replied the senior, and he wiped his aged eyes and walked slowly away.

William started back with horror and instantly recollected his dream. It was indeed the very individual to whose house he was journeying that he now saw laid in his grave. His first duty was to go to the bereaved family of his departed friend, and to comfort the widow and the fatherless. A tear rolled from his manly eye as he entered the mansion of sorrow; and when he saw the relict and the weeping family of his friend he thought his heart would have died within him. Having paid into their hands the money he owed them, and performed various offices of kindness, he bade them for the present adieu, and went to Inverness.

He had no business to transact there; his only object was to obtain the aid of justice in pursuit of the three men whom he supposed to be the murderers. Neil M'Kinnon was apprehended at the house where Laidlaw first saw him; but though his guilt was strongly suspected, no positive proof could be adduced against him, and he was dismissed. The two other men were never heard of. It was supposed that they had gone on board a smuggling cutter which left Fort-William, and afterwards perished, with all its crew, in the Sound of Mull.

The dream still continued to agitate the yeoman's mind to a great degree, and from being the gayest farmer of the Borders, he returned as thoughtful as a philosopher.

MARKHEIM

'Yes,' said the dealer, 'our windfalls are of various kinds. Some customers are ignorant, and then I touch a dividend on my superior knowledge. Some are dishonest,' and here he held up the candle, so that the light fell strongly on his visitor, 'and in that case,' he continued, 'I profit by my virtue.'

Markheim had but just entered from the daylight streets, and his eyes had not yet grown familiar with the mingled shine and darkness in the shop. At these pointed words, and before the near presence of the flame, he blinked painfully and looked aside.

The dealer chuckled. 'You come to me on Christmas day,' he resumed, 'when you know that I am alone in my house, put up my shutters, and make a point of refusing business. Well, you will have to pay for that; you will have to pay for my loss of time, when I should be balancing my books; you will have to pay, besides, for a kind of manner that I remark in you today very strongly. I am the essence of discretion, and ask no awkward questions; but when a customer cannot look me in the eye, he has to pay for it.' The dealer once more chuckled; and then, changing to his usual business voice, though still with a note of irony, 'You can give, as usual, a clear account of how you came into the possession of the object?' he continued. 'Still your uncle's cabinet? A remarkable collector, sir!'

And the little pale, round-shouldered dealer stood almost on tip-toe, looking over the top of his gold spectacles, and nodding his head with every mark of disbelief. Markheim returned his gaze with one of infinite pity, and a touch of horror.

'This time,' said he, 'you are in error. I have not come to sell, but to buy. I have no curios to dispose of; my uncle's cabinet is bare to the wainscot; even were it still intact, I have done well on the Stock Exchange, and should more likely add to it than otherwise, and my errand today is simplicity itself. I seek a Christmas present for a lady,' he continued, waxing more fluent as he struck into the speech he had prepared; 'and certainly I owe you every excuse for thus disturbing you upon so small a matter. But the thing was neglected yesterday; I must produce my little compliment at dinner; and, as you very well know, a rich marriage is not a thing to be neglected.'

There followed a pause, during which the dealer seemed to weigh this statement incredulously. The ticking of many clocks among the curious lumber of the shop, and the faint rushing of the cabs in a near thoroughfare, filled up the interval of silence.

'Well, sir,' said the dealer, 'be it so. You are an old customer after all; and if, as you say, you have the chance of a good marriage, far be it from me to be an obstacle. Here is a nice thing for a lady now,' he went on, 'this hand-glass – fifteenth century, warranted; comes from a good collection, too; but I reserve the name, in the interests of my customer, who was, just like yourself, my dear sir, the nephew and sole heir of a remarkable collector.'

The dealer, while he thus ran on in his dry and biting voice, had stooped to take the object from its place; and, as he had done so, a shock had passed through Markheim, a start both of hand and foot, a sudden leap of many tumultuous passions to the face. It passed as swiftly as it came, and left no trace beyond a certain trembling of the hand that now received the glass.

'A glass,' he said hoarsely, and then paused, and repeated it more clearly. 'A glass? For Christmas? Surely not?'

'And why not?' cried the dealer. 'Why not a glass?'

Markheim was looking upon him with an indefinable expression. 'You ask me why not?' he said. 'Why, look here – look in it – look at yourself! Do you like to see it? No! nor I – nor any man.'

The little man had jumped back when Markheim had so suddenly confronted him with the mirror; but now, perceiving there was nothing worse on hand, he chuckled. 'Your future lady, sir, must be pretty hard favoured,' said he.

'I ask you,' said Markheim, 'for a Christmas present, and you give me this – this damned reminder of years, and sins and follies – this hand-conscience! Did you mean it? Had you a thought in your mind? Tell me. It will be better for you if you do. Come, tell me about yourself. I hazard a guess now, that you are in secret a very charitable man?'

The dealer looked closely at his companion. It was very odd, Markheim did not appear to be laughing; there was something in his face like an eager sparkle of hope, but nothing of mirth.

'What are you driving at?' the dealer asked.

'Not charitable?' returned the other, gloomily. 'Not charitable; not pious; not scrupulous; unloving, unbeloved; a hand to get money, a safe to keep it. Is that all? Dear God, man, is that all?'

'I will tell you what it is,' began the dealer, with some sharpness, and then broke off again into a chuckle. 'But I see this is a love-match of yours, and you have been drinking the lady's health.'

'Ah!' cried Markheim, with a strange curiosity. 'Ah, have you been in love? Tell me about that.'

'I!' cried the dealer. 'I in love! I never had the time, nor have I the time today for all this nonsense. Will you take the glass?'

'Where is the hurry?' returned Markheim. 'It is very pleasant to stand here talking; and my life is so short and insecure that I would not hurry away from any pleasure – no, not even from so mild a one as this. We should rather cling, cling to what little we can get, like a man at a cliff's edge. Every second is a cliff, if you think upon it – a cliff a mile high – high enough, if we fall, to dash us out of every feature of humanity. Hence it is best to talk pleasantly. Let us talk of each other; why should we wear this mask? Let us be confidential. Who knows, we might become friends?'

'I have just one word to say to you,' said the dealer. 'Either make your purchase, or walk out of my shop.'

'True, true,' said Markheim. 'Enough fooling. To business. Show me something else.'

The dealer stooped once more, this time to replace the glass upon the shelf, his thin blond hair falling over his eyes as he did so. Markheim moved a little nearer, with one hand in the pocket of his greatcoat; he drew himself up and filled his lungs; at the same time many different emotions were depicted together on his face – terror, horror, and resolve, fascination and a physical repulsion; and through a haggard lift of his upper lip, his teeth looked out.

'This, perhaps, may suit,' observed the dealer; and then, as he began to re-arise, Markheim bounded from behind upon his victim. The long, skewerlike dagger flashed and fell. The dealer struggled like a hen, striking his temple on the shelf, and then tumbled on the floor in a heap.

Time had some score of small voices in that shop, some stately and slow as was becoming to their great age; others garrulous and hurried. All these told out the seconds in an intricate chorus of tickings. Then the passage of a lad's feet, heavily running on the pavement, broke in upon these smaller voices and startled Markheim into the consciousness of his surroundings. He looked about him awfully. The candle stood on the counter, its flame solemnly wagging in a draught; and by that inconsiderable movement, the whole room was filled with noiseless bustle and kept heaving like a sea: the tall shadows nodding, the gross blots of darkness swelling and dwindling as with respiration, the faces of the portraits and the china gods changing and wavering like images in water. The inner door stood ajar, and peered into that leaguer of shadows with a long slit of daylight like a pointing finger.

From these fear-stricken rovings, Markheim's eyes returned to the body of his victim, where it lay both humped and sprawling, incredibly small and strangely meaner than in life. In these poor, miserly clothes, in that ungainly attitude, the dealer lay like so much sawdust. Markheim had feared to see it, and, lo! it was nothing. And yet, as he gazed, this bundle of old clothes and pool of blood began to find eloquent voices. There it must lie; there was none to work the cunning hinges or direct the miracle of loco-motion – there it must lie till it was found. Found! ay, and then? Then would this dead flesh lift up a cry that would ring over England, and fill the world with the echoes of pursuit. Ay, dead or not, this was still the enemy. 'Time was that when the brains were out,' he thought; and the first word struck into his mind. Time, now that the deed was accomplished – time, which had closed for the victim, had become instant and momentous for the slayer.

The thought was yet in his mind, when, first one and then an-other with every variety of pace and voice – one deep as the bell from a cathedral turret, another ringing on its treble notes the pre-lude of a waltz – the clocks began to strike the hour of three in the afternoon.

The sudden outbreak of so many tongues in that dumb chamber staggered him. He began to bestir himself, going to and fro with the candle, beleaguered by moving shadows, and startled to the soul by chance reflections. In many rich mirrors, some of home de-signs, some from Venice or Amsterdam, he saw his face repeated and repeated, as it were an army of spies; his own eyes met and de-tected him; and the sound of his own steps, lightly as they fell, vexed the surrounding quiet. And still as he continued to fill his pockets, his mind accused him, with a sickening iteration, of the thousand faults of his design. He should have chosen a more quiet hour; he should have prepared an alibi; he should not have used a knife; he should have been more cautious, and only bound and gagged the dealer, and not killed him; he should have been more bold, and killed the servant also; he should have done all things otherwise; poignant regrets, weary, incessant toiling of the mind to change what was unchangeable, to plan what was now useless, to be the architect of the irrevocable past. Meanwhile, and behind all this activity, brute terrors, like the scurrying of rats in a deserted attic; filled the more remote chambers of his brain with riot; the hand of the constable would fall heavy on his shoulder, and his nerves would jerk like a hooked fish; or he beheld, in galloping defile, the dock, the prison, the gallows, and the black coffin.

Terror of the people in the street sat down before his mind like a besieging army. It was impossible, he thought, but that some rumour of the struggle must have reached their ears and set on edge their curiosity; and now, in all the neighbouring houses, he divined them sitting motionless and with uplifted ear – solitary people, condemned to spend Christmas dwelling alone on memories of the past, and now startlingly recalled from that tender exercise; happy family parties, struck into silence round the table, the mother still with raised finger: every degree and age and humour, but all, by their own hearths, prying and hearkening and weaving the rope that was to hang him. Sometimes it seemed to him he could not move too softly; the clink of the tall Bohemian goblets rang out loudly like a bell; and alarmed by the bigness of the ticking, he was tempted to stop the clocks. And then, again, with a swift transition of his terrors, the very silence of the place appeared a source of peril, and a thing to strike and freeze the passer-by; and he would step more boldly, and bustle aloud among the contents of the shop, and imitate, with elaborate bravado, the movements of a busy man at ease in his own house.

But he was now so pulled about by different alarms, that, while one portion of his mind was still alert and cunning, another trembled on the brink of lunacy. One hallucination in particular took a strong hold on his credulity. The neighbour hearkening with white face beside his window, the passer-by arrested by a horrible surmise on the pavement – these could at worst suspect, they could not know; through the brick walls and shuttered windows only sounds could penetrate. But here, within the house, was he alone? He knew he was; he had watched the servant set forth sweethearting, in her poor best, 'out for the day' written in every ribbon and smile. Yes, he was alone, of course; and yet, in the bulk of empty house about him, he could surely hear a stir of delicate footing – he was surely conscious, inexplicably conscious of some presence. Ay, surely; to every room and corner of the house his imagination followed it; and now it was a faceless thing, and yet had eyes to see with; and again it was a shadow of himself; and yet again behold the image of the dead dealer, reinspired with cunning and hatred.

At times, with a strong effort, he would glance at the open door, which still seemed to repel his eyes. The house was tall, the skylight small and dirty, the day blind with fog; and the light that

119

filtered down to the ground storey was exceedingly faint, and showed dimly on the threshold of the shop. And yet, in that strip of doubtful brightness, did there not hang wavering a shadow?

Suddenly, from the street outside, a very jovial gentleman began to beat with a staff on the shop-door, accompanying his blows with shouts and railleries in which the dealer was continually called upon by name. Markheim, smitten into ice, glanced at the dead man. But no! he lay quite still; he was fled away far beyond earshot of these blows and shoutings; he was sunk beneath seas of silence; and his name, which would once have caught his notice above the howling of a storm, had become an empty sound. And presently the jovial gentleman desisted from his knocking and departed.

Here was a broad hint to hurry what remained to be done, to get forth from this accusing neighbourhood, to conscious repugnance of the mind, yet with a tremor of the other side of day, that haven of safety and apparent innocence – his bed. One visitor had come: at any moment another might follow and be more obstinate. To have done the deed, and yet not to reap the profit, would be too abhorrent a failure. The money, that was now Markheim's concern; and as a means to that, the keys.

He glanced over his shoulder at the open door, where the shadow was still lingering and shivering; and with no conscious repugnance of the mind, yet with a tremor of the belly, he drew near the body of his victim. The human character had quite departed. Like a suit half-stuffed with bran, the limbs lay scattered, the trunk doubled, on the floor; and yet the thing repelled him. Although so dingy and inconsiderable to the eye, he feared it might have more significance to the touch. He took the body by the shoulders, and turned it on its back. It was strangely light and supple, and the limbs, as if they had been broken, fell into the oddest postures. The face was robbed of all expression; but it was as pale as wax, and shockingly smeared with blood about one temple. That was, for Markheim, the one displeasing circumstance. It carried him back, upon the instant, to a certain fair day in a fishers' village: a grey day, a piping wind, a crowd upon the street, the blare of brasses, the booming of drums, the nasal voice of a ballad-singer; and a boy going to and fro, buried over head in the crowd and divided between interest and fear, until, coming out upon the chief place of concourse, he beheld a booth and a great screen with pictures, dismally designed, garishly coloured: Brownrigg with her apprentice; the Mannings with their murdered guest; Weare in the death-grip of Thurtell; and a score besides of famous crimes. The thing was as

120

clear as an illusion; he was once again that little boy; he was looking once again, and with the same sense of physical revolt, at these vile pictures; he was still stunned by the thumping of the drums. A bar of that day's music returned upon his memory; and at that, for the first time, a qualm came over him, a breath of nausea, a sudden weakness of the joints, which he must instantly resist and conquer.

He judged it more prudent to confront than to flee from these considerations; looking the more hardily in the dead face, bending his mind to realise the nature and greatness of his crime. So little a while ago that face had moved with every change of sentiment, that pale mouth had spoken, that body had been all on fire with governable energies; and now, and by his act, that piece of life had been arrested, as the horologist, with interjected finger, arrests the beating of the clock. So he reasoned in vain; he could rise to no more remorseful consciousness; the same heart which had shuddered before the painted effigies of crime, looked on its reality unmoved. At best, he felt a gleam of pity for one who had been endowed in vain with all those faculties that can make the world a garden of enchantment, one who had never lived and who was now dead. But of penitence, no, not a tremor.

With that, shaking himself clear of these considerations, he found the keys and advanced towards the open door of the shop. Outside, it had begun to rain smartly; and the sound of the shower upon the roof had banished silence. Like some dripping cavern, the chambers of the house were haunted by an incessant echoing, which filled the ear and mingled with the ticking of the clocks. And, as Markheim approached the door, he seemed to hear, in answer to his own cautious tread, the steps of another foot withdrawing up the stair. The shadow still palpitated loosely on the threshold. He threw a ton's weight of resolve upon his muscles, and drew back the door.

The faint, foggy daylight glimmered dimly on the bare floor and stairs; on the bright suit of armour posted, halbert in hand, upon the landing; and on the dark wood-carvings, and framed pictures that hung against the yellow panels of the wainscot. So loud was the beating of the rain through all the house that, in Markheim's ears, it began to be distinguished into many different sounds. Footsteps and sighs, the tread of regiments marching in the distance, the chink of money in the counting and the creaking of doors held stealthily ajar, appeared to mingle with the patter of the drops upon the cupola and the gushing of the water in the pipes. The sense that he was not alone grew upon him to the verge of mad-

121

ness. On every side he was haunted and begirt by presences. He heard them moving in the upper chambers; from the shop, he heard the dead man getting to his legs; and as he began with a great effort to mount the stairs, feet fled quietly before him and followed stealthily behind. If he were but deaf, he thought, how tranquilly he would possess his soul! And then again, and hearkening with ever fresh attention, he blessed himself for that unresting sense which held the outposts and stood a trusty sentinel upon his life. His head turned continually on his neck; his eyes, which seemed starting from their orbits, scouted on every side, and on every side were half-rewarded as with the tail of something nameless vanishing. The four-and-twenty steps to the first floor were four-and-twenty agonies.

On that first storey, the doors stood ajar, three of them like three ambushes, shaking his nerves like the throats of cannon. He could never again, he felt, be sufficiently immured and fortified from men's observing eyes; he longed to be home, girt in by walls, buried among bedclothes, and invisible to all but God. And at that thought he wondered a little, recollecting tales of other murderers and the fear they were said to entertain of heavenly avengers. It was not so, at least, with him. He feared the laws of nature, lest, in their callous and immutable procedure, they should preserve some damning evidence of his crime. He feared tenfold more, with a slavish, superstitious terror, some scission in the continuity of man's experience, some wilful illegality of nature. He played a game of skill, depending on the rules, calculating consequence from cause; and what if nature, as the defeated tyrant overthrew the chess-board, should break the mould of their succession? The like had befallen Napoleon (so writers said) when the winter changed the time of its appearance. The like might befall Markheim: the solid walls might become transparent and reveal his doings like those of bees in a glass hive; the stout planks might yield under his foot like quicksands and detain him in their clutch; ay, and there were soberer accidents that might destroy him: if, for instance, the house should fall and imprison him beside the body of his victim; or the house next door should fly on fire, and the firemen invade him from all sides. These things he feared; and, in a sense, these things might be called the hands of God reached forth against sin. But about God himself he was at ease; his act was doubtless exceptional, but so were his excuses, which God knew; it was there, and not among men, that he felt sure of justice.

When he had got safe into the drawing-room, and shut the door behind him, he was aware of a respite from alarms. The room was quite dismantled, uncarpeted besides, and strewn with packing-cases and incongruous furniture; several great pier-glasses, in which he beheld himself at various angles, like an actor on a stage; many pictures, framed and unframed, standing, with their faces to the wall; a fine Sheraton sideboard, a cabinet of marquetry, and a great old bed, with tapestry hangings. The windows opened to the floor; but by great good fortune the lower part of the shutters had been closed, and this concealed him from the neighbours. Here, then, Markheim drew in a packing-case before the cabinet, and be-gan to search among the keys. It was a long business, for there were many; and it was irksome, besides; for, after all, there might be nothing in the cabinet, and time was on the wing. But the closeness of the occupation sobered him. With the tail of his eye he saw the door – even glanced at it from time to time directly, like a besieged commander pleased to verify the good estáte of his defences. But in truth he was at peace. The rain falling in the street sounded natural and pleasant. Presently, on the other side, the notes of a piano were wakened to the music of a hymn, and the voices of many children took up the air and words. How stately, how com-fortable was the melody! How fresh the youthful voices! Markheim gave ear to it smilingly, as he sorted out the keys; and his mind was thronged with answerable ideas and images; church-going children and the pealing of the high organ; children afield, bathers by the brookside, ramblers on the brambly common, kite-flyers in the windy and cloud-navigated sky; and then, at another cadence of the hymn, back again to church, and the somnolence of summer Sundays, and the high genteel voice of the parson (which he smiled a little to recall) and the painted Jacobean tombs, and the dim lettering of the Ten Commandments in the chancel.

And as he sat thus, at once busy and absent, he was startled to his feet. A flash of ice, a flash of fire, a bursting gush of blood, went over him, and then he stood transfixed and thrilling. A step mounted the stair slowly and steadily, and presently a hand was laid upon the knob, and the lock clicked, and the door opened.

Fear held Markheim in a vice. What to expect he knew not, whether the dead man walking, or the official ministers of human justice, or some chance witness blindly stumbling in to consign him to the gallows. But when a face was thrust into the aperture, glanced round the room, looked at him, nodded and smiled as if in friendly recognition, and then withdrew again, and the door closed behind it, his fear broke loose from his control in a hoarse cry. At the sound of this the visitant returned.

'Did you call me?' he asked pleasantly, and with that he

entered the room and closed the door behind him.

Markheim stood and gazed at him with all his eyes. Perhaps there was a film upon his sight, but the outlines of the newcomer seemed to change and waver like those of the idols in the wavering candle-light of the shop; and at times he thought he knew him; and at times he thought he bore a likeness to himself; and always, like a lump of living terror, there lay in his bosom the conviction that this thing was not of the earth and not of God.

And yet the creature had a strange air of commonplace as he stood looking on Markheim with a smile; and when he added: 'You are looking for the money, I believe?' it was in the tones of everyday politeness.

Markheim made no answer.

'I should warn you,' resumed the other, 'that the maid has left her sweetheart earlier than usual and will soon be here. If Mr Markheim be found in this house, I need not describe to him the consequences.'

'You know me?' cried the murderer.

The visitor smiled. 'You have long been a favourite of mine,' he said; 'and I have long observed and often sought to help you.'

'What are you?' cried Markheim: 'the devil?'

'What I may be,' returned the other, 'cannot affect the service I propose to render you.'

'It can,' cried Markheim; 'it does! Be helped by you? No, never; not by you! You do not know me yet; thank God, you do not know me!'

'I know you,' replied the visitant, with a sort of kind severity or rather firmness. 'I know you to the soul.'

'Know me!' cried Markheim. 'Who can do so? My life is but a travesty and slander on myself. I have lived to belie my nature. All men do; all men are better than this disguise that grows about and stifles them. You see each dragged away by life, like one whom bravos have seized and muffled in a cloak. If they had their own control – if you could see their faces, they would be altogether different, they would shine out for heroes and saints! I am worse than most; myself is more overlaid; my excuse is known to me and God. But, had I the time, I could disclose myself.'

'To me?' inquired the visitant.

'To you before all,' returned the murderer. 'I supposed you were intelligent. I thought – since you exist – you would prove a reader of the heart. And yet you would propose to judge me by my acts! Think of it; my acts! I was born and I have lived in a land of giants; giants have dragged me by the wrists since I was born out of my mother – the giants of circumstance. And you would judge me by my acts! But can you not look within? Can you not understand that evil is hateful to me? Can you not see within me the clear writing of conscience, never blurred by any wilful sophistry, although too often disregarded? Can you not read me for a thing that surely must be common as humanity – the unwilling sinner?'

'All this is very feelingly expressed,' was the reply, 'but it regards me not. These points of consistency are beyond my province, and I care not in the least by what compulsion you may have been dragged away, so as you are but carried in the right direction. But time flies; the servant delays, looking in the faces of the crowd and at the pictures on the hoardings, but still she keeps moving nearer; and remember, it is as if the gallows itself were striding towards you through the Christmas streets! Shall I help you; I, who know all? Shall I tell you where to find the money?'

'For what price?' asked Markheim.

'I offer you the service for a Christmas gift,' returned the other.

Markheim could not refrain from smiling with a kind of bitter triumph. 'No,' said he, 'I will take nothing at your hands; if I were dying of thirst, and it was your hand that put the pitcher to my lips, I should find the courage to refuse. It may be credulous, but I will do nothing to commit myself to evil.'

'I have no objection to a death-bed repentance,' observed the visitant.

'Because you disbelieve their efficacy!' Markheim cried.

'I do not say so,' returned the other; 'but I look on these things from a different side, and when the life is done my interest falls. The man has lived to serve me, to spread black looks under colour of religion, or to sow tares in the wheat-field, as you do, in a course of weak compliance with desire. Now that he draws so near to his deliverance, he can add but one act of service – to repent, to die smiling, and thus to build up in confidence and hope the more timorous of my surviving followers. I am not so hard a master. Try me. Accept my help. Please yourself in life as you have done hitherto; please yourself more amply, spread your elbows at the board; and when the night begins to fall and the curtains to be drawn, I tell you, for your greater comfort, that you will find it even easy to compound your quarrel with your conscience, and to make a truckling peace with God. I came but now from such a death-bed, and the room was full of sincere mourners, listening to the man's last words: and when I looked into that face, which had been set as a flint against mercy, I found it smiling with hope.'

'And do you, then, suppose me such a creature?' asked Markheim. 'Do you think I have no more generous aspirations than to sin, and sin, and sin, and, at last, sneak into heaven? My heart rises at the thought. Is this, then, your experience of mankind? or is it because you find me with red hands that you presume such baseness? and is this crime of murder indeed so impious as to dry up the very springs of good?'

'Murder is to me no special category,' replied the other. 'All sins are murder, even as all life is war. I behold your race, like starving mariners on a raft, plucking crusts out of the hands of famine and feeding on each other's lives. I follow sins beyond the moment of their acting; I find in all that the last consequence is death; and to my eyes, the pretty maid who thwarts her mother with such taking graces on a question of a ball, drips no less visibly with human gore than such a murderer as yourself. Do I say that I follow sins? I follow virtues also; they differ not by the thickness of a nail, they are both scythes for the reaping angel of Death. Evil, for which I live, consists not in action, but in character. The bad man is dear to me; not the bad act, whose fruits, if we could follow them far enough down the hurtling cataract of the ages, might yet be found more blessed than those of the rarest virtues. And it is not because you have killed a dealer, but because you are Markheim, that I offered to forward your escape.'

'I will lay my heart open to you,' answered Markheim. 'This crime on which you find me is my last. On my way to it I have learned many lessons; itself is a lesson, a momentous lesson. Hitherto I have been driven with revolt to what I would not; I was a bond-slave to poverty, driven and scourged. There are robust virtues that can stand in these temptations; mine was not so: I had a thirst of pleasure. But today, and out of this deed, I pluck both warning and riches – both the power and a fresh resolve to be myself. I become in all things a free actor in the world; I begin to see myself all changed, these hands the agents of good, this heart at peace. Something comes over me out of the past; something of what I have dreamed on Sabbath evenings to the sound of the church organ, of what I forecast when I shed tears over noble books, or talked, an innocent child, with my mother. There lies my life; I have wandered a few years, but now I see once more my city of destination.'

'You are to use this money on the Stock Exchange, I think?' remarked the visitor; 'and there, if I mistake not, you have already lost some thousands?'

'Ah,' said Markheim, 'but this time I have a sure thing.'

'This time, again, you will lose,' replied the visitor quietly.

126

'Ah, but I keep back the half!' cried Markheim.

'That also you will lose,' said the other.

The sweat started upon Markheim's brow. 'Well, then, what matter?' he exclaimed. 'Say it be lost, say I am plunged again in poverty, shall one part of me, and that the worse, continue until the end to override the better? Evil and good run strong in me, haling me both ways. I do not love the one thing, I love all. I can conceive great deeds, renunciations, martyrdoms; and though I be fallen to such a crime as murder, pity is no stranger to my thoughts. I pity the poor; who knows their trials better than myself? I pity and help them; I prize love, I love honest laughter; there is no good thing nor true thing on earth but I love it from my heart. And are my vices only to direct my life, and my virtues to lie without effect, like some passive lumber of the mind? Not so; good, also, is a spring of acts.'

But the visitant raised his finger. 'For six-and-thirty years that you have been in this world,' said he, 'through many changes of fortune and varieties of humour, I have watched you steadily fall. Fifteen years ago you would have started at a theft. Three years back you would have blenched at the name of murder. Is there any crime, is there any cruelty or meanness, from which you still recoil? – five years from now I shall detect you in the fact! Downward, downward, lies your way; nor can anything but death avail to stop you.'

'It is true,' Markheim said huskily, 'I have in some degree complied with evil. But it is so with all: the very saints, in the mere exercise of living, grow less dainty, and take on the tone of their surroundings.'

'I will propound to you one simple question,' said the other; 'and as you answer, I shall read to you your moral horoscope. You have grown in many things more lax; possibly you do right to be so; and at any account, it is the same with all men. But granting that, are you in any one particular, however trifling, more difficult to please with your own conduct, or do you go in all things with a looser rein?'

'In any one?' repeated Markheim, with an anguish of consideration. 'No,' he added, with despair, 'in none! I have gone down in all.'

'Then,' said the visitor, 'content yourself with what you are, for you will never change; and the words of your part on this stage are irrevocably written down.'

Markheim stood for a long while silent, and indeed it was the

127

visitor who first broke the silence. 'That being so,' he said, 'shall I show you the money?'

'And grace?' cried Markheim.

'Have you not tried it?' returned the other. 'Two or three years ago, did I not see you on the platform of revival meetings, and was not your voice the loudest in the hymn?'

'It is true,' said Markheim; 'and I see clearly what remains for me by way of duty. I thank you for these lessons from my soul; my eyes are opened, and I behold myself at last for what I am.'

At this moment, the sharp note of the door-bell rang through the house; and the visitant, as though this were some concerted signal for which he had been waiting, changed at once in his demeanour.

'The maid!' he cried. 'She has returned, as I forewarned you, and there is now before you one more difficult passage. Her master, you must say, is ill; you must let her in, with an assured but rather serious countenance – no smiles, no overacting, and I promise you success! Once the girl within, and the door closed, the same dexterity that has already rid you of the dealer will relieve you of this last danger in your path. Thenceforward you have the whole evening – the whole night, if needful – to ransack the treasures of the house and to make good your safety. This is help that comes to you with the mask of danger. Up!' he cried: 'up, friend; your life hangs trembling in the scales: up, and act!'

Markheim steadily regarded his counsellor. 'If I be condemned to evil acts,' he said, 'there is still one door of freedom open – I can cease from action. If my life be an ill thing, I can lay it down. Though I be, as you say truly, at the beck of every small temptation, I can yet, by one decisive gesture, place myself beyond the reach of all. My love of good is damned to barrenness; it may, and let it be! But I have still my hatred of evil; and from that, to your galling disappointment, you shall see that I can draw both energy and courage.'

The features of the visitor began to undergo a wonderful and lovely change: they brightened and softened with a tender triumph; and, even as they brightened, faded and dislimned. But Markheim did not pause to watch or understand the transformation. He opened the door and went downstairs very slowly, thinking to himself. His past went soberly before him; he beheld it as it was, ugly and strenuous like a dream, random as chance-medley – a scene of defeat. Life, as he thus reviewed it, tempted him no longer; but on the farther side he perceived a quiet haven for his bark. He paused in the passage, and looked into the shop, where the candle still

128

burned by the dead body. It was strangely silent. Thoughts of the dealer swarmed into his mind, as he stood gazing. And then the bell once more broke out into impatient clamour.

He confronted the maid upon the threshold with something like a smile.

'You had better go for the police,' said he: 'I have killed your master.'

W. E. AYTOUN

THE MAN IN THE BELL

IN my younger days bell-ringing was much more in fashion among the young men of —— than it is now. Nobody, I believe, practises it there at present except the servants of the church, and the melody has been much injured in consequence. Some fifty years ago about twenty of us who dwelt in the vicinity of the cathedral formed a club, which used to ring every peal that was called for; and from continual practice and a rivalry which arose between us and a club attached to another steeple, and which tended considerably to sharpen our zeal, we became very Mozarts on our favourite instruments. But my bell-ringing practice was shortened by a singular accident, which not only stopped my performance, but made even the sound of a bell terrible to my ears.

One Sunday I went with another into the belfry to ring for noon prayers, but the second stroke we had pulled showed us that the clapper of the bell we were at was muffled. Some one had been buried that morning, and it had been prepared, of course, to ring a mournful note. We did not know of this, but the remedy was easy.

'Jack,' said my companion, 'step up to the loft and cut off the hat'; for the way we had of muffling was by tying a piece of an old hat, or of cloth (the former was preferred), to one side of the clapper, which deadened every second toll.

I complied, and mounting into the belfry, crept as usual into the bell, where I began to cut away. The hat had been tied on in some more complicated manner than usual, and I was perhaps three or four minutes in getting it off, during which time my companion below was hastily called away, by a message from his sweetheart, I believe; but that is not material to my story.

The person who called him was a brother of the club, who, knowing that the time had come for ringing for service, and not thinking that any one was above, began to pull. At this moment I was just getting out, when I felt the bell moving; I guessed the reason at once – it was a moment of terror; but by a hasty, and almost convulsive effort, I succeeded in jumping down, and throwing myself

130

on the flat of my back under the bell.

The room in which it was was little more than sufficient to contain it, the bottom of the bell coming within a couple of feet of the floor of lath. At that time I certainly was not so bulky as I am now, but as I lay it was within an inch of my face. I had not laid myself down a second when the ringing began. It was a dreadful situation. Over me swung an immense mass of metal, one touch of which would have crushed me to pieces; the floor under me was principally composed of crazy laths, and if they gave way, I was precipitated to the distance of about fifty feet upon a loft, which would, in all probability, have sunk under the impulse of my fall, and sent me to be dashed to atoms upon the marble floor of the chancel, a hundred feet below.

I remembered – for fear is quick in recollection – how a common clock-wright, about a month before, had fallen, and bursting through the floors of the steeple, driven in the ceilings of the porch, and even broken into the marble tombstone of a bishop who slept beneath. This was my first terror, but the ringing had not continued a minute before a more awful and immediate dread came on me. The deafening sound of the bell smote into my ears with a thunder which made me fear their drums would crack. There was not a fibre of my body it did not thrill through! It entered my very soul; thought and reflection were almost utterly banished; I only retained the sensation of agonising terror.

Every moment I saw the bell sweep within an inch of my face and my eyes – I could not close them, though to look at the object was bitter as death – followed it instinctively in its oscillating progress until it came back again. It was in vain I said to myself that it could come no nearer at any future swing than it did at first; every time it descended I endeavoured to shrink into the very floor to avoid being buried under the down-sweeping mass; and then reflecting on the danger of pressing too weightily on my frail support, would cower up again as far as I dared.

At first my fears were mere matter of fact. I was afraid the pulleys above would give way and let the bell plunge on me. At another time the possibility of the clapper being shot out in some sweep, and dashing through my body, as I had seen a ramrod glide through a door, flitted across my mind. The dread also, as I have already mentioned, of the crazy floor, tormented me; but these soon gave way to fears not more unfounded, but more visionary, and of course more tremendous. The roaring of the bell confused my intellect, and my fancy soon began to teem with all sorts of strange and terrifying ideas. The bell pealing above, and opening

131

its jaws with a hideous clamour, seemed to me at one time a ravening monster, raging to devour me; at another, a whirlpool ready to suck me into its bellowing abyss.

As I gazed on it, it assumed all shapes; it was a flying eagle, or rather a roc of the Arabian story-tellers, clapping its wings and screaming over me. As I looked upwards into it, it would appear sometimes to lengthen into indefinite extent, or to be twisted at the end into the spiral folds of the tail of a flying-dragon. Nor was the flaming breath, or fiery glance of that fabled animal, wanting to complete the picture. My eyes, inflamed, bloodshot, and glaring, invested the supposed monster with a full proportion of unholy light.

It would be endless were I to merely hint at all the fancies that possessed my mind. Every object that was hideous and roaring presented itself to my imagination. I often thought that I was in a hurricane at sea, and that the vessel in which I was embarked tossed under me with the most furious vehemence. The air, set in motion by the swinging of the bell, blew over me, nearly with the violence, and more than the thunder of a tempest; and the floor seemed to reel under me, as under a drunken man.

But the most awful of all the ideas that seized on me were drawn from the supernatural. In the vast cavern of the bell hideous faces appeared, and glared down on me with terrifying frowns, or with grinning mockery, still more appalling. At last the devil himself, accoutred, as in the common description of the evil spirit, with hoof, horn, and tail, and eyes of infernal lustre, made his appearance, and called on me to curse God and worship him, who was powerful to save me. This dread suggestion he uttered with the full-toned clangour of the bell. I had him within an inch of me and I thought on the fate of the Santon Barsisa. Strenuously and desperately I defied him, and bade him begone.

Reason then, for a moment, resumed her sway, but it was only to fill me with fresh terror, just as the lightning dispels the gloom that surrounds the benighted mariner, but to show him that his vessel is driving on a rock, where she must inevitably be dashed to pieces. I found I was becoming delirious, and trembled lest reason should utterly desert me. This is at all times an agonising thought, but it smote me then with tenfold agony. I feared lest, when utterly deprived of my senses, I should rise, to do which I was every moment tempted by that strange feeling which calls on a man, whose head is dizzy from standing on the battlement of a lofty castle, to precipitate himself from it, and then death would be instant and tremendous.

When I thought of this I became desperate. I caught the floor with a grasp which drove the blood from my nails; and I yelled with the cry of despair. I called for help, I prayed, I shouted, but all the efforts of my voice were, of course, drowned in the bell. As it passed over my mouth it occasionally echoed my cries, which mixed not with its own sound, but preserved their distinct character. Perhaps this was but fancy. To me, I know, they then sounded as if they were the shouting, howling, or laughing of the fiends with which my imagination had peopled the gloomy cave which swung over me.

You may accuse me of exaggerating my feelings; but I am not. Many a scene of dread have I since passed through, but they are nothing to the self-inflicted terrors of this half hour. The ancients have doomed one of the damned in their Tartarus to lie under a rock, which every moment seems to be descending to annihilate him – and an awful punishment it would be. But if to this you add a clamour as loud as if ten thousand furies were howling about you – a deafening uproar banishing reason, and driving you to madness, you must allow that the bitterness of the pang was rendered more terrible. There is no man, firm as his nerves may be, who could retain his courage in this situation.

In twenty minutes the ringing was done. Half of that time passed over me without power of computation – the other half appeared an age. When it ceased, I became gradually more quiet, but a new fear retained me. I knew that five minutes would elapse without ringing, but at the end of that short time the bell would be rung a second time, for five minutes more. I could not calculate time. A minute and an hour were of equal duration. I feared to rise, lest the five minutes should have elapsed, and the ringing be again commenced, in which case I should be crushed, before I could escape, against the walls or framework of the bell. I therefore still continued to lie down, cautiously shifting myself, however, with a careful gliding, so that my eye no longer looked into the hollow.

This was of itself a considerable relief. The cessation of the noise had, in a great measure, the effect of stupefying me, for my attention, being no longer occupied by the chimeras I had conjured up, began to flag. All that now distressed me was the constant expectation of the second ringing, for which, however, I settled myself with a kind of stupid resolution. I closed my eyes, and clenched my teeth as firmly as if they were screwed in a vice. At last the dreaded moment came, and the first swing of the bell extorted a groan from me, as they say the most resolute victim screams at the sight of the rack, to which he is for a second time destined. After this, however,

133

I lay silent and lethargic, without a thought. Wrapped in the defensive armour of stupidity, I defied the bell and its intonations. When it ceased, I was roused a little by the hope of escape. I did not, however, decide on this step hastily, but, putting up my hand with the utmost caution, I touched the rim.

Though the ringing had ceased, it still was tremulous from the sound, and shook under my hand, which instantly recoiled as from an electric jar. A quarter of an hour probably elapsed before I again dared to make the experiment, and then I found it at rest. I determined to lose no time, fearing that I might have delayed already too long, and that the bell for evening service would catch me. This dread stimulated me, and I slipped out with the utmost rapidity and arose. I stood, I suppose, for a minute, looking with silly wonder on the place of my imprisonment, penetrated with joy of escaping, but then rushed down the stony and irregular stair with the velocity of lightning, and arrived in the bell-ringer's room. This was the last act I had power to accomplish. I leaned against the wall, motionless and deprived of thought, in which posture my companions found me, when, in the course of a couple of hours, they returned to their occupation.

They were shocked, as well they might, at the figure before them. The wind of the bell had excoriated my face, and my dim and stupefied eyes were fixed with a lack-lustre gaze in my raw eyelids. My hands were torn and bleeding, my hair dishevelled, and my clothes tattered. They spoke to me, but I gave no answer. They shook me, but I remained insensible. They then became alarmed, and hastened to remove me. He who had first gone up with me in the forenoon met them as they carried me through the churchyard, and through him, who was shocked at having, in some measure, occasioned the accident, the cause of my misfortune was discovered. I was put to bed at home, and remained for three days delirious, but gradually recovered my senses.

You may be sure the bell formed a prominent topic of my ravings, and if I heard a peal, they were instantly increased to the utmost violence. Even when the delirium abated, my sleep was continually disturbed by imagined ringings, and my dreams were haunted by the fancies which almost maddened me while in the steeple. My friends removed me to a house in the country, which was sufficiently distant from any place of worship to save me from the apprehensions of hearing the church-going bell; for what Alexander Selkirk, in Cowper's poem, complained of as a misfortune, was then to me as a blessing.

Here I recovered; but, even long after recovery, if a gale wafted the notes of a peal towards me, I started with nervous apprehension. I felt a Mahometan hatred to all the bell tribe, and envied the subjects of the Commander of the Faithful the sonorous voice of their Muezzin' Time cured this, as it does the most of our follies; but, even at the present day, if, by chance, my nerves be unstrung, some particular tones of the cathedral bell have power to surprise me into a momentary start.

THE TWO DROVERS

I

IT WAS the day after Doune Fair when my story commences. It had been a brisk market, several dealers had attended from the northern and midland counties in England, and English money had flown so merrily about as to gladden the hearts of the High-land farmers. Many large droves were about to set off for England, under the protection of their owners, or of the topsmen whom they employed in the tedious, laborious, and responsible office of driving the cattle for many hundred miles, from the market where they had been purchased, to the fields or farm-yards where they were to be fattened for the shambles.

The Highlanders, in particular, are masters of this difficult trade of driving, which seems to suit them as well as the trade of war. It affords excercise for all their habits of patient endurance and active exertion. They are required to know perfectly the drove-roads, which lie over the wildest tracts of the country, and to avoid as much as possible the highways, which distress the feet of the bullocks, and the turnpikes, which annoy the spirit of the drover; whereas, on the broad green or grey track, which leads across the pathless moor, the herd not only move at ease and without taxa-tion, but, if they mind their business, may pick up a mouthful of food by the way. At night, the drovers usually sleep along with their cattle, let the weather be what it will, and many of these hardy men do not once rest under a roof during a journey on foot from Lochaber to Lincolnshire. They are paid very highly, for the trust reposed is of the last importance, as it depends on their prudence, vigilance, and honesty, whether the cattle reach the final market in good order, and afford a profit to the grazier. But as they main-tain themselves at their own expense, they are especially econ-omical in that particular. At the period we speak of, a Highland drover was victualled for his long and toilsome journey with a few handfuls of oatmeal, and two or three onions, renewed from time to time, and a ram's horn filled with whisky, which he used regularly, but sparingly, every night and morning. His dirk, or *skene-dhu* (i.e. black-knife), so worn as to be concealed beneath the arm, or by the folds of the plaid, was his only weapon, excepting the cudgel with which he directed the movements of the cattle. A Highlander was never so happy as on these occasions. There was a variety in the whole journey, which exercised the Celt's natural curiosity and love of motion; there were the constant change of place and scene, the petty adventures incidental to the traffic, and the intercourse with the various farmers, graziers, and traders, intermingled with occasional merry-makings, not the less acceptable to Donald that they were void of expense – and there was the consciousness of superior skill; for the Highlander, a child amongst flocks, is a prince amongst herds, and his natural habits induce him to disdain the shepherd's slothful life, so that he feels himself nowhere more at home than when following a gallant drove of his country cattle in the character of their guardian.

Of the number who left Doune in the morning, and with the purpose we described, not a *Glunamie* of them all cocked his bonnet more briskly, or gartered his tartan hose under knee over a pair of more promising *spiogs* (legs) than did Robin Oig M'Combich, called familiarly Robin Oig, that is, Young, or the Lesser, Robin. Though small of stature as the epithet Oig implies, and not very strongly limbed, he was as light and alert as one of the deer of his mountains. He had an elasticity of step which, in the course of a long march, made many a stout fellow envy him; and the manner in which he busked his plaid and adjusted his bonnet, argued a consciousness that so smart a John Highlandman as himself would not pass unnoticed among the Lowland lasses. The ruddy cheek, red lips, and white teeth, set off a countenance which had gained by exposure to the weather a healthful and hardy rather than a rugged hue. If Robin Oig did not laugh, or even smile frequently, as indeed is not the practice among his countrymen, his bright eyes usually gleamed from under his bonnet with an expression of cheerfulness ready to be turned into mirth.

The departure of Robin Oig was an incident in the little town, in and near which he had many friends, male and female. He was a topping person in his way, transacted considerable business on his own behalf, and was entrusted by the best farmers in the Highlands in preference to any other drover in that district. He might have increased his business to any extent had he condescended to manage it by deputy; but except a lad or two, sister's sons of his own, Robin rejected the idea of assistance, conscious, perhaps, how much his reputation depended upon his attending in person to the practical discharge of his duty in every instance. He remained, therefore, contented with the highest premium given to persons of his description, and comforted himself with the hopes that a few journeys to England might enable him to conduct business on his own account, in a manner becoming his birth. For Robin Oig's father, Lachlan M'Combich (or *son of my friend*, his actual clan-surname being M'Gregor), had been so called by the celebrated Rob Roy, because of the particular friendship which had subsisted between the grandsire of Robin and that renowned cateran. Some people even say that Robin Oig derived his Christian name from one as renowned in the wilds of Loch Lomond as ever was his namesake Robin Hood, in the precincts of merry Sherwood. 'Of such ancestry', as James Boswell says, 'who would not be proud?' Robin Oig was proud accordingly; but his frequent visits to England and to the Lowlands had given him tact enough to know that pretensions, which still gave him a little right to distinction in his own lonely glen, might be both obnoxious and ridiculous if preferred elsewhere. The pride of birth, therefore, was like the miser's treasure, the secret subject of his contemplation, but never exhibited to strangers as a subject of boasting.

Many were the words of gratulation and good luck which were bestowed on Robin Oig. The judges commended his drove, especially Robin's own property, which were the best of them. Some thrust out their snuff-mulls for the parting pinch – others tendered the *doch-an-dorrach* or parting cup. All cried – 'Good luck travel out with you and come home with you. – Give you luck in the Saxon market – brave notes in the *leabhar-dhu*' (black pocket-book) 'and plenty of English gold in the *sporran*' (pouch of goatskin).

The bonny lasses made their adieus more modestly, and more than one, it was said, would have given her best brooch to be certain that it was upon her that his eye last rested as he turned towards the road.

Robin Oig had just given the preliminary '*Hoo-hoo!*' to urge forward the loiterers of the drove, when there was a cry behind him.

'Stay, Robin – bide a blink. Here is Janet of Tomahourich – auld Janet, your father's sister.'

'Plague on her, for an auld Highland witch and spaewife,' said a farmer from the Carse of Stirling; 'she'll cast some of her cantrips on the cattle.'

'She canna do that,' said another sapient of the same profession – 'Robin Oig is no the lad to leave any of them without tying St Mungo's knot on their tails, and that will put to her speed the best witch that ever flew over Dimayet upon a broomstick.'

It may not be indifferent to the reader to know that the Highland cattle are peculiarly liable to be *taken*, or infected, by spells and witchcraft; which judicious people guard against by knitting knots of peculiar complexity on the tuft of hair which terminates the animal's tail.

But the old woman who was the object of the farmer's suspicion seemed only busied about the drover, without paying any attention to the drove. Robin, on the contrary, appeared rather impatient of her presence.

'What auld-world fancy,' he said, 'has brought you so early from the ingle-side this morning, Muhme? I am sure I bid you good-even, and had your God-speed, last night.'

'And left me more siller than the useless old woman will use till you come back again, bird of my bosom,' said the sibyl. 'But it is little I would care for the food that nourishes me, or the fire that warms me, or for God's blessed sun itself, if aught but weel should happen to the grandson of my father. So let me walk the *deasil* round you, that you may go safe out into the foreign land, and come safe home.'

Robin Oig stopped, half embarrassed, half laughing, and signing to those near that he only complied with the old woman to soothe her humour. In the meantime she traced around him, with wavering steps, the propitiation, which some have thought has been derived from the Druidical mythology. It consists, as is well known, in the person who makes the *deasil* walking three times round the person who is the object of the ceremony, taking care to move according to the course of the sun. At once, however, she stopped short, and exclaimed, in a voice of alarm and horror, 'Grandson of my father, there is blood on your hand.'

'Hush, for God's sake, aunt,' said Robin Oig; 'you will bring more trouble on yourself with this Taishataragh' (second sight) 'than you will be able to get out of for many a day.'

The old woman only repeated, with a ghastly look, 'There is blood on your hand, and it is English blood. The blood of the Gael is richer and redder. Let us see – let us –'

Ere Robin Oig could prevent her, which, indeed, could only have been done by positive violence, so hasty and peremptory were her proceedings, she had drawn from his side the dirk which lodged in the folds of his plaid, and held it up, exclaiming, although the weapon gleamed clear and bright in the sun, 'Blood, blood – Saxon blood again. Robin Oig M'Combich, go not this day to England!'

'Prutt, trutt,' answered Robin Oig, 'that will never do neither – it would be next thing to running the country. For shame, Muhme – give me the dirk. You cannot tell by the colour the difference betwixt the blood of a black bullock and a white one, and you speak of knowing Saxon from Gaelic blood. All men have their blood from Adam, Muhme. Give me my skene-dhu, and let me go on my road. I should have been half-way to Stirling Brig by this time. – Give me my dirk, and let me go.'

'Never will I give it to you,' said the old woman. – 'Never will I quit my hold on your plaid, unless you promise me not to wear that unhappy weapon.'

The women around him urged him also, saying few of his aunt's words fell to the ground; and as the Lowland farmers continued to look moodily on the scene, Robin Oig determined to close it at any sacrifice.

'Well, then,' said the young drover, giving the scabbard of the weapon to Hugh Morrison, 'you Lowlanders care nothing for these freats. Keep my dirk for me. I cannot give it to you, because it was my father's; but your drove follows ours, and I am content it should be in your keeping, not in mine. – Will this do, Muhme?'

'It must,' said the old woman – 'that is, if the Lowlander is mad enough to carry the knife.'

The strong westlandman laughed aloud.

'Goodwife,' said he, 'I am Hugh Morrison from Glenae, come of the Manly Morrisons of auld langsyne, that never took short weapon against a man in their lives. And neither needed they. They had their broadswords, and I have this bit supple,' showing a formidable cudgel – 'for dirking ower the board, I leave that to John Highlandman. – Ye needna snort, none of you Highlanders, and you in especial, Robin. I'll keep the bit knife, if you are feared for the auld spaewife's tale, and give it back to you whenever you want it.'

Robin was not particularly pleased with some part of Hugh Morrison's speech; but he had learned in his travels more patience than belonged to his Highland constitution originally, and he accepted the service of the descendant of the Manly Morrisons without finding fault with the rather depreciating manner in which it was offered.

'If he had not had his morning in his head, and been but a Dumfriesshire hog into the boot, he would have spoken more like a gentleman. But you cannot have more of a sow than a grumph. It's shame my father's knife should ever slash a haggis for the like of him.'

140

Thus saying (but saying it in Gaelic) Robin drove on his cattle, and waved farewell to all behind him. He was in the greater haste, because he expected to join at Falkirk a comrade and brother in profession, with whom he proposed to travel in company.

Robin Oig's chosen friend was a young Englishman, Harry Wakefield by name, well known at every northern market, and in his way as much famed and honoured as our Highland driver of bullocks. He was nearly six feet high, gallantly formed to keep the rounds at Smithfield, or maintain the ring at a wrestling match; and although he might have been overmatched, perhaps, among the regular professors of the Fancy, yet, as a yokel, or rustic, or a chance customer, he was able to give a bellyful to any amateur of the pugilistic art. Doncaster races saw him in his glory, betting his guinea, and generally successfully; nor was there a main fought in Yorkshire, the feeders being persons of celebrity, at which he was not to be seen, if business permitted. But though a *sprack* lad, and fond of pleasure and its haunts, Harry Wakefield was steady, and not the cautious Robin Oig M'Combich himself was more attentive to the main chance. His holidays were holidays indeed; but his days of work were dedicated to steady and persevering labour. In countenance and temper, Wakefield was the model of old England's merry yeomen, whose clothyard shafts, in so many hundred battles, asserted her superiority over the nations, and whose good sabres in our own time are her cheapest and most assured defence. His mirth was readily excited; for, strong in limb and constitution, and fortunate in circumstances, he was disposed to be pleased with everything about him; and such difficulties as he might occasionally encounter were, to a man of his energy, rather matter of amusement than serious annoyance. With all the merits of a sanguine temper, our young English drover was not without his defects. He was irascible, sometimes to the verge of being quarrelsome; and perhaps not the less inclined to bring his disputes to a pugilistic decision, because he found few antagonists able to stand up to him in the boxing ring.

It is difficult to say how Harry Wakefield and Robin Oig first became intimates; but it is certain a close acquaintance had taken place betwixt them, although they had apparently few common subjects of conversation or of interest, so soon as their talk ceased to be of bullocks. Robin Oig, indeed, spoke the English language rather imperfectly upon any other topics but stots and kyloes, and Harry Wakefield could never bring his broad Yorkshire tongue to utter a single word of Gaelic. It was in vain Robin spent a whole morning, during a walk over Minch Moor in attempting to teach his companion to utter, with true precision, the shibboleth *Llhu*, which is the Gaelic for a calf. From Traquair to Murdercairn, the hill rang with the discordant attempts of the Saxon upon the unmanageable monosyllable, and the heartfelt laugh which followed every failure. They had, however, better modes of awakening the echoes; for Wakefield could sing many a ditty to the praise of Moll, Susan, and Cicely, and Robin Oig had a particular gift at whistling interminable pibrochs through all their involutions, and what was more agreeable to his companion's southern ear, knew many of the northern airs, both lively and pathetic, to which Wakefield learned to pipe a bass. This, though Robin could hardly have comprehended his companion's stories about horse-racing, and cock-fighting or fox-hunting, and although his own legends of clan-fights and *creaghs*, varied with talk of Highland goblins and fairy folk, would have been caviare to his companion, they contrived nevertheless to find a degree of pleasure in each other's company, which had for three years back induced them to join company and travel together, when the direction of their journey permitted. Each, indeed, found his advantage in this companionship; for where could the Englishman have found a guide through the Western Highlands like Robin Oig M'Combich? and when they were on what Harry called the *right* side of the Border, his patronage, which was extensive, and his purse, which was heavy, were at all times in the service of his Highland friend, and on many occasions his liberality did him genuine yeoman's service.

II

Were ever two such loving friends! –
How could they disagree?
O thus it was, he loved him dear,
And thought how to requite him,
And having no friend left but he,
He did resolve to fight him.

Duke upon Duke

The pair of friends had traversed with their usual cordiality the grassy wilds of Liddesdale, and crossed the opposite part of Cumberland, emphatically called The Waste. In these solitary regions, the cattle under the charge of our drovers derived their subsistence chiefly by picking their food as they went along the drove-road, or sometimes by the tempting opportunity of a *start and owerloup*, or invasion of the neighbouring pasture, where an occasion presented itself. But now the scene changed before them; they were descending towards a fertile and enclosed country, where no such liberties could be taken with impunity, or without a previous arrangement and bargain with the possessors of the ground. This was more especially the case, as a great northern fair was upon the eve of taking place, where both the Scotch and English drover expected to dispose of a part of their cattle, which it was desirable to produce in the market, rested and in good order. Fields were therefore difficult to be obtained, and only upon high terms. This necessity occasioned a temporary separation betwixt the two friends, who went to bargain, each as he could, for the separate accommodation of his herd. Unhappily it chanced that both of them, unknown to each other, thought of bargaining for the ground they wanted on the property of a country gentleman of some fortune, whose estate lay in the neighbourhood. The English drover applied to the bailiff on the property, who was known to him. It chanced that the Cumbrian squire, who had entertained some suspicions of his manager's honesty, was taking occasional measures to ascertain how far they were well founded, and had desired that any inquiries about his enclosures, with a view to occupy them for a temporary purpose, should be referred to himself. As, however, Mr Ireby had gone the day before upon a journey of some miles' distance to the northward, the bailiff chose to consider the check upon his full powers as for the time removed, and concluded that he should best consult his master's interest, and perhaps his own, in making an agreement with Harry Wakefield. Meanwhile, ignorant of what his comrade was doing, Robin Oig, on his side, chanced to be overtaken by a good-looking smart little man upon a pony, most knowingly hogged and cropped, as was then the fashion, the rider wearing tight leather breeches and long-necked bright spurs. This cavalier asked one or two pertinent questions about markets and the price of stock. So Robin, seeing him a well-judging civil gentleman, took the freedom to ask him whether he could let him know if there was any grass-land to be let in that neighbourhood, for the temporary accommodation of his drove. He could not have put the question to more willing ears. The gentlemen of the buckskin was the proprietor with whose bailiff Harry Wakefield had dealt or was in the act of dealing.

'Thou art in good luck, my canny Scot,' said Mr Ireby, 'to have spoken to me, for I see thy cattle have done their day's work, and I have at my disposal the only field within three miles that is to be let in these parts.'

'The drove can pe gang two, three, four miles very pratty weel indeed,' said the cautious Highlander; 'put what would his honour be axing for the peasts pe the head, if she was to tak the park for twa or three days?'

'We won't differ, Sawney, if you let me have six stots for winterers, in the way of reason.'

'And which peasts wad your honour pe for having?'

'Why – let me see – the two black – the dun one – yon doddy – him with the twisted horn – the brockit – How much by the head?'

'Ah,' said Robin, 'your honour is a shudge – a real shudge – I couldna have set off the pest six peasts petter mysell, me that ken them as if they were my pairns, puir things.'

'Well, how much per head, Sawney?' continued Mr Ireby.

'It was high markets at Doune and Falkirk,' answered Robin.

And thus the conversation proceeded, until they had agreed on the *prix juste* for the bullocks, the squire throwing in the temporary accommodation of the enclosure for the cattle into the boot, and Robin making, as he thought, a very good bargain, provided the grass was but tolerable. The squire walked his pony alongside of the drove, partly to show him the way, and see him put into possession of the field, and partly to learn the latest news of the northern markets.

They arrived at the field, and the pasture seemed excellent. But what was their surprise when they saw the bailiff quietly inducting the castle of Harry Wakefield into the grassy Goshen which had just been assigned to those of Robin Oig M'Combich by the proprietor himself! Squire Ireby set spurs to his horse, dashed up to his servant, and learning what had passed between the parties, briefly informed the English drover that his bailiff had let the ground without his authority, and that he might seek grass for his cattle wherever he would, since he was to get none there. At the same time he rebuked his servant severely for having transgressed his commands, and ordered him instantly to assist in ejecting the hungry and weary cattle of Harry Wakefield, which were just beginning to enjoy a meal of unusual plenty, and to introduce those of his comrade, whom the English drover now began to consider as a rival.

The feelings which arose in Wakefield's mind would have induced him to resist Mr Ireby's decision; but every Englishman has a tolerably accurate sense of law and justice, and John Fleecebumpkin, the bailiff, having acknowledged that he had exceeded his commission, Wakefield saw nothing else for it than to collect his hungry and disappointed charge, and drive them on to seek quarters elsewhere. Robin Oig saw what had happened with regret, and hastened to offer to his English friend to share with him the disputed possession. But Wakefield's pride was severely hurt, and he answered disdainfully, 'Take it all, man – take it all – never make two bites of a cherry – thou canst talk over the gentry, and blear a plain man's eye – Out upon you, man – I would not kiss any man's dirty latchets for leave to bake in his oven.'

Robin Oig, sorry but not surprised at his comrade's displeasure, hastened to entreat his friend to wait but an hour till he had gone to the squire's house to receive payment for the cattle he had sold, and he could come back and help him to drive the cattle into some convenient place of rest, and explain to him the whole mistake they had both of them fallen into. But the Englishman continued indignant: 'Thou hast been selling, hast thou? Ay, ay – thou is a cunning lad for kenning the hours of bargaining. Go to the devil with thyself, for I will ne'er see thy fause loon's visage again – thou should be ashamed to look me in the face.'

'I am ashamed to look no man in the face,' said Robin Oig, something moved; 'and, moreover, I will look you in the face this blessed day, if you will bide at the clachan down yonder.'

'Mayhap you had as well keep away,' said his comrade; and turning his back on his former friend, he collected his unwilling associates, assisted by the bailiff, who took some real and some affected interest in seeing Wakefield accommodated.

After spending some time in negotiating with more than one of the neighbouring farmers, who could not, or would not, afford the accommodation desired, Henry Wakefield at last, and in his necessity, accomplished his point by means of the landlord of the ale-house at which Robin Oig and he had agreed to pass the night, when they first separated from each other. Mine host was content to let him turn his cattle on a piece of barren moor, at a price little less than the bailiff had asked for the disputed enclosure; and the wretchedness of the pasture, as well as the price paid for it, were set down as exaggerations of the breach of faith and friendship of his Scottish crony. This turn of Wakefield's passions was encouraged by the bailiff (who had his own reasons for being offended against poor Robin, as having been the unwitting cause of his falling into disgrace with his master), as well as by the innkeeper, and two or three chance guests, who stimulated the drover in his resentment against his quondam associate, – some from the ancient grudge against the Scots which, when it exists anywhere, is to be found lurking in the Border counties, and some from the general love of mischief, which characterises mankind in all ranks of life, to the honour of Adam's children be it spoken. Good John Barley-corn also, who always heightens and exaggerates the prevailing passions, be they angry or kindly, was not wanting in his offices on this occasion; and confusion to false friends and hard masters was pledged in more than one tankard.

In the meanwhile Mr Ireby found some amusement in detain-ing the northern drover at his ancient hall. He caused a cold round of beef to be placed before the Scot in the butler's pantry, together with a foaming tankard of home-brewed, and took pleasure in seeing the hearty appetite with which these unwonted edibles were discussed by Robin Oig M'Combich. The squire himself lighting his pipe, compounded between his patrician dignity and his love of agricultural gossip, by walking up and down while he con-versed with his guest.

'I passed another drove,' said the squire, 'with one of your countrymen behind them – they were something less beasts than you drove, doddies most of them – a big man was with them – none of your kilts though, but a decent pair of breeches – D'ye know who he may be?'

'Hout aye – that might, could, and would be Hughie Morrison – I didna think he could hae peen sae weel up. He has made a day on us; but his Argyleshires will have wearied shanks. How far was he pehind.'

'I think about six or seven miles,' answered the squire, 'for I passed them at the Christenbury Crag, and I overtook you at the Hollan Bush. If his beasts be leg-weary, he will maybe be selling bargains.'

'Na, na, Hughie Morrison is no the man for pargains – ye maun come to some Highland body like Robin Oig hersell for the like of these – put I maun pe wishing you goot night, and twenty of them 'et alane ane, and I maun down to the clachan to see if the lad Harry Waakfelt is out of his humdudgeons yet.'

The party at the alehouse was still in full talk, and the treachery of Robin Oig still the theme of conversation, when the supposed culprit entered the apartment. His arrival, as usually happens in such a case, put an instant stop to the discussion of which he had furnished the subject, and he was received by the company assembled with that chilling silence which, more than a thousand exclamations, tells an intruder that he is unwelcome. Surprised and offended, but not appalled by the reception which he experienced, Robin entered with an undaunted and even a haughty air, at-tempted no greeting as he saw he was received with none, and placed himself by the side of the fire, a little apart from a table at

146

which Harry Wakefield, the bailiff, and two or three other persons were seated. The ample Cumbrian kitchen would have afforded plenty of room, even for a larger separation.

Robin, thus seated, proceeded to light his pipe, and call for a pint of twopenny.

'We have no twopence ale,' answered Ralph Heskett, the land-lord; 'but as thou findest thy own tobacco, it's like thou mayest find thy own liquor too – it's the wont of thy country, I wot.'

'Shame, goodman,' said the landlady, a blithe bustling house-wife, hastening herself to supply the guest with liquor – 'Thou knowest well enow what the strange man wants, and it's thy trade to be civil, man. Thou shouldst know, that if the Scot likes a small pot, he pays a sure penny.'

Without taking any notice of this nuptial dialogue, the High-lander took the flagon in his hand, and addressing the company generally, drank the interesting toast of 'Good markets', to the party assembled.

'The better that the wind blew fewer dealers from the north,' said one of the farmers, 'and fewer Highland runts to eat up the English meadows.'

'Saul of my pody, put you are wrang there, my friend,' answered Robin, with composure, 'it is your fat Englishmen that eat up our Scots cattle, puir things.'

'I wish there was a summat to eat up their drovers,' said another; 'a plain Englishman canna make bread within a kenning of them.'

'Or an honest servant keep his master's favour, but they will come sliding in between him and the sunshine,' said the bailiff.

'If these pe jokes,' said Robin Oig, with the same composure, 'there is ower mony jokes upon one man.'

'It is no joke, but downright earnest,' said the bailiff. 'Harkye, Mr Robin Ogg, or whatever is your name, it's right we should tell you that we are all of one opinion, and that is that you, Mr Robin Ogg, have behaved to our friend Mr Harry Wakefield here, like a raff and a blackguard.'

'Nae doubt, nae doubt,' answered Robin, with great com-posure; 'and you are a set of very pretty judges, for whose prains or pehaviour I wad not gie a pinch of sneeshing. If Mr Harry Waak-felt kens where he is wranged, he kens where he may be righted.'

'He speaks truth,' said Wakefield, who had listened to what passed, divided between the offence which he had taken at Robin's late behaviour, and the revival of his habitual feelings of regard. He now arose, and went towards Robin, who got up from his seat as he approached, and held out his hand.

'That's right, Harry – go it – serve him out,' resounded on all sides – 'tip him the nailer – show him the mill.'

'Hold your peace all of you, and be –,' said Wakefield; and then addressing his comrade, he took him by the extended hand, with something alike of respect and defiance. 'Robin,' he said, 'thou hast used me ill enough this day; but if you mean, like a frank fellow, to shake hands, and make a tussle for love on the sod, why I'll forgie thee, man, and we shall be better friends than ever.'

'And would it not pe petter to pe cood friends without more of the matter?' said Robin; 'we will be much petter friendships with our panes hale than proken.'

Harry Wakefield dropped the hand of his friend, or rather threw it from him.

'I did not think I had been keeping company for three years with a coward.'

'Coward pelongs to none of my name,' said Robin, whose eyes began to kindle, but keeping the command of his temper. 'It was no coward's legs or hands, Harry Waakfelt, that drew you out of the fords of Frew, when you was drifting ower the plack rock, and every eel in the river expected his share of you.'

'And that is true enough, too,' said the Englishman, struck by the appeal.

'Adzooks!' exclaimed the bailiff – 'sure Harry Wakefield, the nattiest lad at Whitson Tryste, Wooler Fair, Carlisle Sands, or Stagshaw Bank, is not going to show white feather? Ah, this comes of living, so long with kilts and bonnets – men forget the use of their daddles.'

'I may teach you, Master Fleecebumpkin, that I have not lost the use of mine,' said Wakefield, and then went on. 'This will never do, Robin. We must have a turn-up, or we shall be the talk of the country-side. I'll be d – d if I hurt thee – I'll put on the gloves gin thou like. Come, stand forward like a man.'

'To pe peaten like a dog,' said Robin; 'is there any reason in that? If you think I have done you wrong, I'll go before your shudge, though I neither know his law nor his language.'

A general cry of 'No, no – no law, no lawyer! a bellyful and be friends,' was echoed by the bystanders.

'But,' continued Robin, 'if I am to fight, I've no skill to fight like a jackanapes, with hands and nails.'

'How would you fight, then?' said his antagonist; 'though I am thinking it would be hard to bring you to the scratch anyhow.'

'I would fight with proadswords, and sink point on the first

148

plood drawn, like a gentleman.'

A loud shout of laughter followed the proposal, which indeed had rather escaped from poor Robin's swelling heart, than been the dictate of his sober judgement.

'Gentleman, quotha!' was echoed on all sides, with a shout of unextinguishable laughter; 'a very pretty gentleman, God wot – Canst get two swords for the gentlemen to fight with, Ralph Heskett?'

'No, but I can send to the armoury at Carlisle, and lend them two forks, to be making shift with in the meantime.'

'Tush, man,' said another, 'the bonny Scots come into the world with the blue bonnet on their heads, and dirk and pistol at their belt.'

'Best send post,' said Mr Fleecebumpkin, 'to the squire of Corby Castle, to come and stand second to the *gentleman*.'

In the midst of this torrent of general ridicule, the Highlander instinctively griped beneath the folds of his plaid.

'But it's better not,' he said in his own language. 'A hundred curses on the swine-eaters, who know neither decency nor civility!'

'Make room, the pack of you,' he said, advancing to the door.

But his former friend interposed his sturdy bulk, and opposed his leaving the house; and when Robin Oig attempted to make his way by force, he hit him down on the floor, with as much ease as a boy bowls down a nine-pin.

'A ring, a ring!' was now shouted, until the dark rafters, and the hams that hung on them, trembled again, and the very platters on the *bink* clattered against each other. 'Well done, Harry' – 'Give it him home, Harry' – 'Take care of him now – he sees his own blood!'

Such were the exclamations, while the Highlander, starting from the ground, all his coldness and caution lost in frantic rage, sprang at his antagonist with the fury, the activity, and the vindictive purpose of an incensed tiger-cat. But when could rage encounter science and temper? Robin Oig again went down in the unequal contest; and as the blow was necessarily a severe one, he lay motionless on the floor of the kitchen. The landlady ran to offer some aid, but Mr Fleecebumpkin would not permit her to approach.

'Let him alone,' he said, 'he will come to within time, and come up to the scratch again. He has not got half his broth yet.'

'He has got all I mean to give him, though,' said his antagonist, whose heart began to relent towards his old associate; 'and I would rather by half give the rest to yourself, Mr Fleecebumpkin, for you pretend to know a thing or two, and Robin had not art enough even to peel before setting to, but fought with his plaid dangling about him. – Stand up, Robin, my man! all friends now; and let me hear the man that will speak a word against you, or your country, for your sake.'

Robin Oig was still under the dominion of his passion, and eager to renew the onset; but being withheld on the one side by the peace-making Dame Heskett, and on the other, aware that Wakefield no longer meant to renew the combat, his fury sank into gloomy sullenness.

'Come, come, never grudge so much at it, man,' said the brave-spirited Englishman, with the placability of his country, 'shake hands, and we will be better friends than ever.'

'Friends!' exclaimed Robin Oig, with strong emphasis – 'friends! – Never. Look to yourself, Harry Waakfelt.'

'Then the curse of Cromwell on your proud Scots stomach, as the man says in the play, and you may do your worst, and be d – ; for one man can say nothing more to another after a tussle, than that he is sorry for it.'

On these terms the friends parted; Robin Oig drew out, in silence, a piece of money, threw it on the table, and then left the alehouse. But turning at the door, he shook his hand at Wakefield, pointing with his forefinger upwards, in a manner which might imply either a threat or a caution. He then disappeared in the moonlight.

Some words passed after his departure between the bailiff, who piqued himself on being a little of a bully, and Harry Wakefield, who, with generous inconsistency, was now not indisposed to begin a new combat in defence of Robin Oig's reputation, 'although he could not use his daddles like an Englishman, as it did not come natural to him.' But Dame Heskett prevented this second quarrel from coming to a head by her peremptory interference. 'There should be no more fighting in her house,' she said; 'there had been too much already .– And you, Mr Wakefield, may live to learn', she added, 'what it is to make a deadly enemy out of a good friend.'

'Pshaw, dame! Robin Oig is an honest fellow, and will never keep malice.'

'Do not trust to that – you do not know the dour temper of the Scots, though you have dealt with them so often. I have a right to know them, my mother being a Scot.'

'And so is well seen on her daughter,' said Ralph Heskett.

This nuptial sarcasm gave the discourse another turn; fresh

customers entered the tap-room or kitchen, and others left it. The conversation turned on the expected markets, and the report of prices from different parts both of Scotland and England – treaties were commenced, and Harry Wakefield was lucky enough to find a chap for a part of his drove, and at a very considerable profit; an event of consequence more than sufficient to blot out all remembrances of the unpleasant scuffle in the earlier part of the day. But there remained one party from whose mind that recollection could not have been wiped away by the possession of every head of cattle betwixt Esk and Eden.

This was Robin Oig M'Combich. – 'That I should have had no weapon,' he said, 'and for the first time in my life! – Blighted be the tongue that bids the Highlander part with the dirk – the dirk – ha! the English blood! – My Muhme's word – when did her word fall to the ground?'

The recollection of the fatal prophecy confirmed the deadly intention which instantly sprang up in his mind.

'Ha! Morrison cannot be many miles behind; and if it were a hundred, what then?'

His impetuous spirit had now a fixed purpose and motive of action, and he turned the light foot of his country towards the wilds, through which he knew, by Mr Ireby's report, that Morrison was advancing. His mind was wholly engrossed by the sense of injury – injury sustained from a friend; and by the desire of vengeance on one whom he now accounted his most bitter enemy. The treasured ideas of self-importance and self-opinion – of ideal birth and quality, had become more precious to him (like the hoard to the miser) because he could only enjoy them in secret. But that hoard was pillaged, the idols which he had secretly worshipped had been desecrated and profaned. Insulted, abused, and beaten, he was no longer worthy, in his own opinion, of the name he bore or the lineage which he belonged to – nothing was left to him – nothing but revenge; and, as the reflection added a galling spur to every step, he determined it should be as sudden and signal as the offence.

When Robin Oig left the door of the ale-house, seven or eight English miles at least lay betwixt Morrison and him. The advance of the former was slow, limited by the sluggish pace of his cattle; the last left behind him stubble-field and hedge-row, crag and dark heath, all glittering with frost-rime in the broad November moonlight, at the rates of six miles an hour. And now the distant lowing of Morrison's cattle is heard; and now they are seen creeping like moles in size and slowness of motion on the broad face of

151

the moor; and now he meets them – passes them, and stops their conductor.

'May good betide us,' said the Southlander. 'Is this you, Robin M'Combich, or your wraith?'

'It is Robin Oig M'Combich,' answered the Highlander, 'and it is not. – But never mind that, put pe giving me the skene-dhu.'

'What! you are for back to the Highlands – The devil! – Have you selt all off before the fair? This beats all for quick markets!'

'I have not sold – I am not going north – May pe I will never go north again. – Give me pack my dirk, Hugh Morrison, or there will pe words petween us.'

'Indeed, Robin, I'll be better advised before I gie it back to you – it is a wanchancy weapon in a Highlandman's hand, and I am thinking you will be about some barns-breaking.'

'Prutt, trutt! let me have my weapons,' said Robin Oig, impatiently.

'Hooly, and fairly,' said his well-meaning friend. 'I'll tell you what will do better than these dirking doings – Ye ken Highlander, and Lowlander, and Border-men, are a' ae man's bairns when you are over the Scots dyke. See, the Eskdale callants, and fighting Charlie of Liddesdale, and the Lockerby lads, and the four Dandies of Lustruther, and a wheen mair grey plaids, are coming up behind, and if you are wranged, there is the hand of a Manly Morrison, we'll see you righted, if Carlisle and Stanwix baith took up the feud.'

'To tell you the truth,' said Robin Oig, desirous of eluding the suspicions of his friend, 'I have enlisted with a party of the Black Watch, and must march off to-morrow morning.'

'Enlisted! Were you mad or drunk? – You must buy yourself off – I can lend you twenty notes, and twenty to that, if the drove sell.'

'I thank you – thank ye, Hughie; but I go with good will the gate that I am going, – so the dirk – the dirk!'

'There it is for you then, since less wunna serve. But think on what I was saying. – Waes me, it will be sair news in the braes of Balquidder, that Robin Oig M'Combich should have run an ill gate, and ta'en on.'

'Ill news in Balquidder, indeed!' echoed poor Robin. 'But Cot speed you, Hughie, and send you good marcats. Ye winna meet with Robin Oig again, either at tryste or fair.'

So saying, he shook hastily the hand of his acquaintance, and set out in the direction from which he had advanced, with the spirit of his former pace.

'There is something wrang with the lad,' muttered the Morrison to himself, 'but we'll maybe see better into the morn's morning.'

But long ere the morning dawned, the catastrophe of our tale had taken place. It was two hours after the affray had happened, and it was totally forgotten by almost every one, when Robin Oig returned to Heskett's inn. The place was filled at once by various sorts of men, and with noises corresponding to their character. There were the grave low sounds of men engaged in busy traffic, with the laugh, the song, and the riotous jest of those who had nothing to do but to enjoy themselves. Among the last was Harry Wakefield, who, amidst a grinning group of smock-frocks, hob-nailed shoes, and jolly English physiognomies, was trolling forth the old ditty,

What though my name be Roger,
Who drives the plough and cart –

when he was interrupted by a well-known voice saying in a high and stern tone, marked by the sharp Highland accent, 'Harry Waakfelt – if you be a man, stand up!'

'What is the matter? – what is it?' the guests demanded of each other.

'It is only a d – d Scotsman,' said Fleecebumpkin, who was by this time very drunk, 'whom Harry Wakefield helped to his broth the day, who is now come to have *his cauld kail* het again.'

'Harry Waakfelt,' repeated the same ominous summons, 'stand up, if you be a man!'

There is something in the tone of deep and concentrated passion, which attracts attention and imposes awe, even by the very sound. The guests shrank back on every side, and gazed at the Highlander as he stood in the middle of them, his brows bent, and his features rigid with resolution.

'I will stand up with all my heart, Robin, my boy, but it shall be to shake hands with you, and drink down all unkindness. It is not the fault of your heart, man, that you don't know how to clench your hands.'

But this time he stood opposite to his antagonist; his open and unsuspecting look strangely contrasted with the stern purpose, which gleamed wild, dark, and vindictive in the eyes of the Highlander.

' 'Tis not thy fault, man, that, not having the luck to be an Englishman, thou canst not fight more than a schoolgirl.'

'I *can* fight,' answered Robin Oig, sternly but calmly, 'and you shall know it. You, Harry Waakfelt, showed me today how the

153

Saxon churls fight – I show you now how the Highland Dunniè-wassel fights.'

He seconded the word with the action, and plunged the dagger, which he suddenly displayed, into the broad chest of the English yeoman, with such fatal certainty and force, that the hilt made a hollow sound against the breast-bone, and the double-edged point split the very heart of his victim. Harry Wakefield fell and expired with a single groan. His assassin next seized the bailiff by the collar, and offered the bloody poniard to his throat, whilst dread and surprise rendered the man incapable of defence.

'It were very just to lay you beside him,' he said, 'but the blood of a base pick-thank shall never mix on my father's dirk with that of a brave man.'

As he spoke, he cast the man from him with so much force that he fell on the floor, while Robin, with his other hand, threw the fatal weapon into the blazing turf-fire.

'There,' he said, 'take me who likes – and let fire cleanse blood if it can.'

The pause of astonishment still continuing, Robin Oig asked for a peace-officer, and a constable having stepped out, he surrendered himself to his custody.

'A bloody night's work you have made of it,' said the constable.

'Your own fault,' said the Highlander. 'Had you kept his hands off me twa hours since, he would have been now as well and merry as he was twa minutes since.'

'It must be sorely answered,' said the peace-officer.

'Never mind that – death pays all debts; it will pay that too.'

The horror of the bystanders began now to give way to indignation; and the sight of a favourite companion murdered in the midst of them, the provocation being, in their opinion, so utterly inadequate to the excess of vengeance, might have induced them to kill the perpetrator of the deed even upon the very spot. The constable, however, did his duty on this occasion, and with the assistance of some of the more reasonable persons present, procured horses to guard the prisoner to Carlisle, to abide his doom at the next assizes. While the escort was preparing, the prisoner neither expressed the least interest nor attempted the slightest reply. Only, before he was carried from the fatal apartment, he desired to look at the dead body, which, raised from the floor, had been deposited upon the large table (at the head of which Harry Wakefield had presided but a few minutes before, full of life, vigour, and animation) until the surgeons should examine the mortal wound. The face of the corpse was decently covered with a napkin. To the surprise and horror of the bystanders, which displayed itself in a general *Ah!* drawn through clenched teeth and half-shut lips, Robin Oig removed the cloth, and gazed with a mournful but steady eye on the lifeless visage, which had been so lately animated that the smile of good-humoured confidence in his own strength, of conciliation at once and contempt towards his enemy, still curled his lip. While those present expected that the wound, which had so lately flooded the apartment with gore, would send forth fresh streams at the touch of the homicide, Robin Oig replaced the covering with the brief exclamation – 'He was a pretty man!'

My story is nearly ended. The unfortunate Highlander stood his trial at Carlisle. I was myself present, and as a young Scottish lawyer, or barrister at least, and reputed a man of some quality, the politeness of the Sheriff of Cumberland offered me a place on the bench. The facts of the case were proved in the manner I have related them; and whatever might be at first the prejudice of the audience against a crime so un-English as that of assassination from revenge, yet when the rooted national prejudices of the prisoner had been explained, which made him consider himself as stained with indelible dishonour when subjected to personal violence; when his previous patience, moderation, and endurance were considered, the generosity of the English audience was inclined to regard his crime as the wayward aberration of a false idea of honour rather than as flowing from a heart naturally savage, or perverted by habitual vice. I shall never forget the charge of the venerable judge to the jury, although not at that time liable to be much affected either by that which was eloquent or pathetic.

'We have had,' he said, 'in the previous part of our duty' (alluding to some former trials) 'to discuss crimes which infer disgust and abhorrence, while they call down the well-merited vengeance of the law. It is now our still more melancholy task to apply its salutary though severe enactments to a case of a very singular character, in which the crime (for a crime it is, and a deep one) arose less out of the malevolence of the heart, than the error of the understanding – less from an idea of committing wrong, than from an unhappily perverted notion of that which is right. Here we have two men, highly esteemed, it has been stated, in their rank of life, and attached, it seems, to each other as friends, one of whose lives has been already sacrificed to a punctilio, and the other is about to prove the vengeance of the offended laws; and yet both may claim our commiseration at least, as men acting in ignorance of each other's national prejudices, and unhappily misguided rather than voluntarily erring from the path of right conduct.

'In the original cause of the misunderstanding, we must in justice give the right to the prisoner at the bar. He had acquired possession of the enclosure, which was the object of competition, by a legal contract with the proprietor, Mr Ireby; and yet, when accosted with reproaches undeserved in themselves, and galling doubtless to a temper at least sufficiently susceptible of passion, he offered notwithstanding to yield up half his acquisition for the sake of peace and good neighbourhood, and his amicable proposal was rejected with scorn. Then follows the scene at Mr Heskett the publican's, and you will observe how the stranger was treated by the deceased, and, I am sorry to observe, by those around, who seem to have urged him in a manner which was aggravating in the highest degree. While he asked for peace and for composition, and offered submission to a magistrate, or to a mutual arbiter, the prisoner was insulted by a whole company, who seem on this occasion to have forgotten the national maxim of 'fair play'; and while attempting to escape from the place in peace, he was intercepted, struck down, and beaten to the effusion of his blood.

'Gentlemen of the jury, it was with some impatience that I heard my learned brother, who opened the case for the crown, give an unfavourable turn to the prisoner's conduct on this occasion. He said the prisoner was afraid to encounter his antagonist in fair fight, or to submit to the laws of the ring; and that therefore, like a cowardly Italian, he had recourse to his fatal stiletto, to murder the man whom he dared not meet in manly encounter. I observed the prisoner shrink from this part of the accusation with the abhorrence natural to a brave man; and as I would wish to make my words impressive when I point his real crime, I must secure his opinion of my impartiality, by rebutting everything that seems to me a false accusation. There can be no doubt that the prisoner is a man of resolution – too much resolution – I wish to Heaven that he had less, or rather that he had had a better education to regulate it.

'Gentlemen, as to the laws my brother talks of, they may be known in the bull-ring, or the bear-garden, or the cockpit, but they are not known here. Or, if they should be so far admitted as furnishing a species of proof that no malice was intended in this sort of combat, from which fatal accidents do sometimes arise, it can only be so admitted when both parties are *in pari casu*, equally acquainted with, and equally willing to refer themselves to, that species of arbitrament. But will it be contended that a man of superior rank and education is to be subjected, or is obliged to subject himself, to this coarse and brutal strife, perhaps in opposition to

156

a younger, stronger, or more skilful opponent? Certainly even the pugilistic code, if founded upon the fair play of Merry Old England, as my brother alleges it to be, can contain nothing so preposterous. And, gentlemen of the jury, if the laws would support an English gentleman, wearing, we will suppose, his sword, in defending himself by force against a violent personal aggression of the nature offered to this prisoner, they will not less protect a foreigner and a stranger, involved in the same unpleasing circumstances. If, therefore, gentlemen of the jury, when thus pressed by a *vis major*, the object of obloquy to a whole company, and of direct violence from one at least, and, as he might reasonably apprehend, from more, the panel had produced the weapon which his countrymen, as we are informed, generally carry about their persons, and the same unhappy circumstance had ensued which you have heard detailed in evidence, I could not in my conscience have asked from you a verdict of murder. The prisoner's personal defence might, indeed, even in that case, have gone more or less beyond the *Moderamen inculpatae tutelae*, spoken of by lawyers, but the punishment incurred would have been that of manslaughter, not of murder. I beg leave to add that I should have thought this milder species of charge was demanded in the case supposed, notwithstanding the statute of James I cap. 8, which takes the case of slaughter by stabbing with a short weapon, even without malice prepense, out of the benefit of clergy. For this statute of stabbing, as it is termed, arose out of a temporary cause; and as the real guilt is the same, whether the slaughter be committed by the dagger, or by sword or pistol, the benignity of the modern law places them all on the same, or nearly the same footing.

'But, gentlemen of the jury, the pinch of the case lies in the interval of two hours interposed betwixt the reception of the injury and the fatal retaliation. In the heat of affray and *chaude melée*, law, compassionating the infirmities of humanity, makes allowance for the passions which rule such a stormy moment – for the sense of present pain, for the apprehension of further injury, for the difficulty of ascertaining with due accuracy the precise degree of violence which is necessary to protect the person of the individual, without annoying or injuring the assailant more than is absolutely requisite. But the time necessary to walk twelve miles, however speedily performed, was an interval sufficient for the prisoner to have recollected himself; and the violence with so many circumstances of deliberate determination, could neither be induced by the passion of anger, nor that of fear. It was the purpose and the act of predetermined revenge, for which law neither can, will, nor ought to have sympathy or allowance.

'It is true, we may repeat to ourselves, in alleviation of this poor man's unhappy action, that his case is a very peculiar one. The country which he inhabits was, in the days of many now alive, inaccessible to the laws, not only of England, which have not even yet penetrated thither, but to those to which our neighbours of Scotland are subjected, and which must be supposed to be, and no doubt actually are, founded upon the general principles of justice and equity which pervade every civilised country. Amongst their mountains, as among the North American Indians, the various tribes were wont to make war upon each other, so that each man was obliged to go armed for his protection. These men, from the ideas which they entertained of their own descent and of their own consequence, regarded themselves as so many cavaliers or men-at-arms, rather than as the peasantry of a peaceful country. Those laws of the ring, as my brother terms them, were unknown to the race of warlike mountaineers; that decision of quarrels by no other weapons than those which nature has given every man, must to them have seemed as vulgar and as preposterous as to the noblesse of France. Revenge, on the other hand, must have been as familiar to their habits of society as to those of the Cherokees or Mohawks. It is indeed, as described by Bacon, at bottom a kind of wild untutored justice; for the fear of retaliation must withhold the hands of the oppressor where there is no regular law to check daring violence. But though all this may be granted, and though we may allow that, such having been the case of the Highlands in the days of the prisoner's fathers, many of the opinions and sentiments must still continue to influence the present generation, it cannot, and ought not, even in this most painful case, to alter the administration of the law, either in your hands, gentlemen of the jury, or in mine. The first object of civilisation is to place the general protection of the law, equally administered, in the room of that wild justice, which every man cut and carved for himself, according to the length of his sword and the strength of his arm. The law says to the subjects, with a voice only inferior to that of the Deity, "Vengeance is mine." The instant that there is time for passion to cool, and reason to interpose, an injured party must become aware that the law assumes the exclusive cognisance of the right and wrong betwixt the parties, and opposes her inviolable buckler to every attempt of the private party to right himself. I repeat, that this unhappy man ought personally to be the object rather of our pity than our abhorrence, for he failed in his ignorance, and from mistaken notions of honour. But his crime is not the less that of murder, gentlemen, and, in your high and important office, it is your duty so to find. Englishmen have their angry passions as well as Scots; and should this man's action remain unpunished, you may unsheath, under various pretences, a thousand daggers betwixt the Land's-end and the Orkneys.'

The venerable judge thus ended what, to judge by his apparent emotion, and by the tears which filled his eyes, was really a painful task. The jury, according to his instructions, brought in a verdict of Guilty; and Robin Oig M'Combich, *alias* M'Gregor, was sentenced to death and left for execution, which took place accordingly. He met his fate with great firmness, and acknowledged the justice of his sentence. But he repelled indignantly the observations of those who accused him of attacking an unarmed man. 'I give a life for the life I took,' he said, 'and what can I do more?'

NEL BESTSELLERS

Crime

T005 801	RIFIFI IN NEW YORK	*Auguste le Breton* 30p
W002 750	FIVE RED HERRINGS	*Dorothy L. Sayers* 30p
W002 848	CLOUDS OF WITNESS	*Dorothy L. Sayers* 35p
W002 845	THE DOCUMENTS IN THE CASE	*Dorothy L. Sayers* 30p
W003 011	GAUDY NIGHT	*Dorothy L. Sayers* 40p
W002 870	BLOODY MAMA	*Robert Thom* 25p

Fiction

T009 548	SUEDEHEAD	*Richard Allen* 25p
W002 755	PAID SERVANT	*E. R. Braithwaite* 30p
T007 030	A TIME OF PREDATORS	*Joe Gores* 30p
T009 084	SIR, YOU BASTARD	*G. F. Newman* 30p
T009 769	THE HARRAD EXPERIMENT	*Robert H. Rimmer* 40p
T010 716	THE ZOLOTOV AFFAIR	*Robert H. Rimmer* 30p
T010 252	THE REBELLION OF YALE MARRATT	*Robert H. Rimmer* 40p
W002 918	THE ADVENTURERS	*Harold Robbins* 75p
T011 798	A STONE FOR DANNY FISHER	*Harold Robbins* 60p
T011 771	NEVER LOVE A STRANGER	*Harold Robbins* 70p
W002 653	THE DREAM MERCHANTS	*Harold Robbins* 60p
T011 801	WHERE LOVE HAS GONE	*Harold Robbins* 70p
T010 406	NEVER LEAVE ME	*Harold Robbins* 30p
T006 743	THE INHERITORS	*Harold Robbins* 60p
T009 467	STILETTO	*Harold Robbins* 30p
W002 792	THE KILLER	*Colin Wilson* 35p
W002 822	GILLIAN	*Frank Yerby* 40p
W002 479	AN ODOUR OF SANCTITY	*Frank Yerby* 50p
W002 860	FAIROAKS	*Frank Yerby* 40p

Science Fiction

W002 844	STRANGER IN A STRANGE LAND	*Robert Heinlein* 60p
T009 696	GLORY ROAD	*Robert Heinlein* 40p
W002 838	BETWEEN PLANETS	*Robert Heinlein* 30p

War

W002 686	DEATH OF A REGIMENT	*John Foley* 30p
W002 484	THE FLEET THAT HAD TO DIE	*Richard Hough* 25p
W002 805	HUNTING OF FORCE Z	*Richard Hough* 30p
W002 423	STRIKE FROM THE SKY—THE BATTLE OF BRITAIN STORY	*Alexander McKee* 30p

Western

T007 340	TWO RODE NORTH	*J. D. Brady* 25p
T010 619	EDGE—THE LONER	*George Gilman* 25p
T010 600	EDGE—TEN THOUSAND DOLLARS AMERICAN	*George Gilman* 25p

General

T011 763	SEX MANNERS FOR MEN	*Robert Chartham* 30p
W002 531	SEX MANNERS FOR ADVANCED LOVERS	*Robert Chartham* 25p
T010 732	THE SENSUOUS COUPLE	*Dr 'C'* 25p
T007 022	NEW FEMALE SEXUALITY	*Manfred F. De Martino* 50p
W002 584	SEX MANNERS FOR SINGLE GIRLS	*Dr. Georges Valensin* 25p
W002 592	THE FRENCH ART OF SEX MANNERS	*Dr. Georges Valensin* 25p

NEL P.O. BOX 11, FALMOUTH, CORNWALL

Please send cheque or postal order. Allow 5p per book to cover postage and packing (Overseas 6p per book).

Name..

Address ....

....

Title ....
(DECEMBER)